REASONS

THE DICK

--- PULLING THREADS ---

Book Seven

SHERYLL O'BRIEN

This is a work of fiction. All characters in this book are the product of an overactive imagination. Any businesses, organizations, places, events, and incidents are used fictionally. Any resemblance to a real person, living or dead, is a tremendous coincidence.

ISBN 978-1-939351-15-9

WOODWIND PRESS

Printed in United States of America

Mom,

I love the time we spend
talking about my characters ---
as though they are
our friends.

ACKNOWLEDGMENT

To my sister, Marjorie. I know you think you grew up in my shadow – but that's only because you weren't paying attention to what the sun was showing off behind you.

A heartfelt thank you to my team:

Andria Flores ~ Editor extraordinaire.
Nancy Pendleton ~ Goddess of the publishing world.
Jessica Champion ~ Web designer and manager.
25 Hours Consulting
Daryl Bruinsma ~ Cover Design & Animation.

Testimonials

"One book will set the hook!" ~ Nancy Pendleton

"This avid reader predicts that Sheryll O'Brien will become your favorite author. She's mine." ~ Ruth S. Bodreau

"The characters draw you in immediately. You will worry, laugh, hope, and love right along with them." ~ Donna Eaton

"There is nothing sweeter than a Sunday morning coffee, a blanket, overcast skies, and a *Pulling Threads* novel." ~ Andria Flores

"Everything you'd want in a good book. Humor, romance, suspense and great characters! It even takes place by the ocean! Loved it." ~ Helena Green

"I could write a book about the wonderfulness of it all." ~ Faith Lavallee

"Hunks, humor, and heartache! What more could you ask for?" ~ Marjorie McCarthy

"*Bullet Bungalow* is a page turning family saga and then *Netti Barn* and *Cutters Cove* come along and add a whole lot of trauma to the drama." ~ Jessica O'Brien

"The most promising new author I've encountered in my publishing career!" ~ Jim P. - Woodwind Press

--- Pulling Threads ---

Bullet Bungalow
Netti Barn
Cutters Cove
They Run
They Hide
They Choose

PENOBSCOT BAY
A Rocco Fiancetti Incorporated Investigation

Reasons

Coming soon...

Rescues
Resolutions
Torment
Tango
Tests
Resolve
Revenge
Rebound

--- Twisted Threads ---

Coming soon...

Her Scream
Stay Safe

An Important Note from the Editor:

If you've been reading Sheryll's novellas in sequential order, you'll want to get a little clarifying information before you read the first word of *Reasons*. Here's why…

When you turned the last page of *Penobscot Bay*, it was May 2019 and all of our favorite characters were living at The Fiancetti Compound. Book 7 in the Pulling Threads series is going to present some important backstory, and lay the groundwork for the remaining novellas.

Reasons will begin in the year 2003. You will be introduced to a young Manuel and his father, Alistair Duff, (you know him best as Rocco Fiancetti). Several new characters will fill the pages and will help drive the series forward. Trust me — *Reasons* is the catalyst for some explosive storyline with characters who will become a part of your life in the same way that Kitt and Fred, Maura and Steve, John and Joy, and Mike and Annie have!

Think of *Reasons* this way; you are getting 'dirt' from your girlfriend over coffee. Fill your cup, and lean in. When you turn the last page, Sheryll will have brought us all safely back to the year 2019. The thing is, unlike your girlfriend – who would dish in past tense – Sheryll is presenting most of the story in present tense because that's her favorite writing-style. As her editor, I didn't bother arguing with this genius storyteller. So sit back and enjoy *Reasons*.

Reasons

Book 1

Rocco Fiancetti
Manuel Xavier
Sage Finley
Malcolm Price

2003 - 2006

Rocco and Manuel

2003

In a matter of minutes, a handful of royal family members and a respectable showing of nobility will be led into York Minster Cathedral to bid farewell to Lady Frances Duff, better known to the people who love her as, The Duff. The rarified group of 'mourners' would be elsewhere had they their druthers, or dare say a backbone – but they surrendered both to the queen, long ago. And so on this splendid June morn, the appropriately appareled and perfectly pinched upper crusters tread down the center aisle of a spectacular gothic structure known as the Heart of Yorkshire. Flanked on either side of the traversing aisle are rows and rows of precisely spaced and perfectly placed wooden chairs occupied by, "The riffraff with whom Frances associated." It is said that those disparaging words were uttered from on high, but Mum's the word, righto?

Lady Frances Duff, elder daughter of the 2nd Duchess of Waverly, was cast asunder by Her Majesty in the late 1960s for the high crime of bucking the palace and banging a street artist who lay down his brush long enough to lay the lady. The dalliance caused the royal lot to sever ties with The Duff a scant few months before her Dufflet was born. When Frances flew her gilded cage it was said that she took up residence on the streets of London. A more apt telling is that she moved into a lovely garden-terraced flat, began donating her time to worthy causes, sharing her considerable coffers with the neediest souls, and offering her heart to her son, Alistair. Many throughout England considered Frances a paragon of virtue, a doer of good deeds, and one hell of a lady. The royals on the other hand did their best to not consider her at all.

From time to time, however, The Duff would darken the palace doorstep and pull an occasional string or two if it benefited a cause close to her heart. That pulling was not without charge and was most often met with the tightening of the royal noose permanently looped around her neck. Today's funeral of Lady Frances Duff is the culmination of string pulling and rope tightening. Suffice it to say, The Duff would never have consented to this showing had she her druthers, but she surrendered those a long time ago on behalf of her son—the one who is nowhere near the Heart of Yorkshire.

Vienna
Manuel Duff, 13-year-old son of Alistair Duff, sits cross-legged on his twin bed in his residence

room at Mozart International, a prestigious music and art academy located in Vienna's 18th district. Sitting cross-legged on the other twin bed is Manuel's father, a man the kid knows little about, and hasn't seen in nearly a year. The teen trains his eyes on the visitor, casually runs his hand through his shaggy brown hair, and laughs.

The exceedingly handsome man across from the aggravator offers a wide smile that cuts his cheeks with deep dimples and lights his dark eyes with enjoyment — in spite of the reason for his visit. "You are about to comment on the graying at my temples."

"Oh, yeah," the kid sniggers.

"Tread carefully, Manuel."

"Don't think so, old man," the kid laughs.

"Enjoy yourself, but be forewarned. Premature graying is hereditary."

That comment deserves a scoff from the adolescent – it gets one. "Wouldn't know since I haven't a clue about my family, and the one I did know about is dead."

The two Duffs settle into their sorrow and resume watching a news account of the funeral procession of the woman each considers to be their mother. For the elder male, that is a fact of biology, for the adolescent male, it's more a fact of…

London, England
1990

Alistair placed his son into his mother's arms, "You can help by agreeing to the following. You will be guardian of my son and raise him as you did me."

"Alistair," Frances exhaled his name.

"This arrangement is contingent upon the following. You assure my acceptance here at MI6. The only favor I expect is immediate entrance into the training programs. If I do not carry my weight, then I expect to be released from service. I will stay in London and see my boy when I am allowed. These terms are non-negotiable."

Frances Duff used a good measure of her royal sway that afternoon. With babe in arms she stood and nodded to MI6 Senior Special Operative Mick Bentley. "Make it so." She kissed the top of her son's head as he kissed his own boy's, then the lady walked away with Manuel Duff.

"Dad."

"Son."

"I think it's time that you tell me about Rocco Fiancetti."

Alistair was a bit knocked back – Rocco, on the other hand, casually took the incoming. "You, first."

"What?"

"Tell me what **you** know about Rocco Fiancetti."

"I heard The Duff mention him to Mick."

"Proceed."

"I think he might be a relative, someone she worried about."

The father turned toward the television, his breath catching at the sight of his mother's casket being carried into York Minster Cathedral. "We will talk, Manuel. Let me get the door first."

"No one knocked on the door. You're losing it old man."

The international spy pulls open the door and greets the arriving man. "Richard."

"Alistair."

"Maverick."

"Rocco."

The men embrace then enter the very tight quarters.

"Rocco? Rocco? You're Rocco Fiancetti?" the teen stammers.

"About that," the men say.

Did you say, shagging?

Maverick Cross, formerly known as Richard Barrington III, sits in a first-class seat on a London to Cleveland non-stop flight. In the seat next to him is a sullen 13-year-old. Maverick stretches his long legs into the aisle and pushes back into his seat. "There are better ways to spend your time, Manuel."

"Like what?"

"This flight lasts another eight hours. I'm fucking stuck with you for the duration."

"So."

"So you could be bugging the shit out of me for answers about your old man."

A light of dawning shines bright upon the sullen one. "And you'll answer them?"

"Some."

"When did you meet Alistair?"

"We were classmates at Wetherby and then at Ludgrove."

"Are you a royal?"

Maverick snorts his derision, "Bloody no. Could barely tolerate being in lot with the upper crusters let alone with the crownies. Alistair is as close as I ever wanted to get to that royal lot."

"So my grandmother was a lady?"

"Yeah, one hell of a lady. She was bawdy as all get out and took not one bit of shit from anyone."

"You got a story about The Duff?"

Maverick eyes the kid, "How old are you?"

"Thirteen."

"Have you shagged yet?"

"No. Is that a requirement for hearing a story about The Duff?"

Maverick laughs big, "No. Just wanted to know how close an eye I need to keep on you when we settle in."

Manuel joined in on the laugh. "How about I let you know when shagging is in my future."

"Deal. The Duff's story begins with her shagging a young artist who was in England with his uncle," Maverick leans close, "The uncle was an international jewel thief who was visiting his lady friend for a bit of shagging of his own."

"Right," Manuel raises a skeptical brow. "So, where were the artist and jewel thief visiting from?"

"Italy. Why?"

Manuel shrugs a shoulder and smiles wide, "Just wondering how far I should travel for a good shag."

"For a great shag – across the globe. For a good shag – across a continent. For a shag that will do – across town." Maverick's laughter catches the eye of a flight attendant who's already made overtures toward the long haired, bearded brute of a man. He winks at the blue eyed, dirty-blonde, uniformed lovely, then nudges Manuel's shoulder, "I'll be back."

A dawning smirk crosses the kid's face as he grabs his backpack from under his feet. He takes out his iPod, puts in a set of earplugs, and cranks his library of Maverick Cross tunes. He's nearly through the collection of Best Of recordings when his chaperone returns – when his **very happy** chaperone returns. Manuel gives his head a good shake and offers a quick laugh. He fidgets with his iPod a bit, and continues with the shake of his head.

"Got something to say, kid?"

"I'm a bit fucked if you're the best my father could do by way of a guardian."

"Righto, mate."

Manuel puts his gear away and picks up their conversation where they'd left off. "Before your bit of sky-high shagging you were telling me about The Duff."

"In the late 60s the lady got tossed from the kingdom."

"Because she got pregnant with my father?"

"Because she wouldn't tell the royal lot who knocked her knickers."

"Why didn't she tell?"

"There really wasn't much to tell. The Duff and the artist met, did the deed, and went their separate ways."

"Like you and the stewardess, over there."

"Let's hope not," Maverick laughs. "Anyway, it was several years before she told the artist their dalliance resulted in a kid. By then, the painter had made a name for himself and wasn't interested in the whole 'daddy thing'. When Alistair pushed to meet his old man, The Duff arranged vacations for the three of them along the French and Italian Rivieras. The Duff put her feelings aside, her life on hold, and got the mates together."

Manuel is quiet for a minute. "You were right."

"About?"

"The Duff was one hell of a lady."

Manuel turns his pain toward the tiny window. At that moment, high above the clouds and as near to The Duff as he'd ever felt, he whispers the word, "Xavier."

"What?"

"My father said I could choose my last name, now that I can't use Duff anymore."

"Xavier," Maverick repeats. "Manuel Xavier. It's got a good ring to it. Why Xavier?"

"The Duff listened to Xavier Cugat non-stop. She liked the mambo." The grieving grandson closes his teary eyes and whispers, "Manuel Xavier."

2005

Assistant Inspector General of British cyber intelligence, Mick Bentley, has been standing at the office door of MI6 Special Operative, Alistair Duff, for several minutes. The **man** is staring out at the River Thames, seemingly unaware of his boss' presence – the **spy** is well-aware. "Are you here for a reason, AIG Bentley?"

"If the reason was to off you, Alistair, you'd be long dead."

"One of us would be," the Special Operative continues his look-about, addressing his boss and best friend over his shoulder, "Something on your mind, Mick?"

"Same thing that's on your mind, I suppose."

"Eleni..."

Genoa, Italy
1989

Rocco exited the Fiancetti heat studio needing relief from the sweltering box. Sweat droplets rolled down his face and chest onto steamy brick inlay at his feet. The bib of his jean overalls hung at his waist – caked with that day's sweat and dust. Sinewy, exaggerated muscles ran his arms, having been raised from the brute work at the kiln. The overheated man pulled a long breath, found no relief in the stifling, stagnant air. The handkerchief he pulled from his back pocket drenched quickly as he wiped his face and neck.

"You work a kiln?"

Rocco turned quickly and found the keeper of the voice; an exquisite wonder standing at the end of the brick alleyway. "Si."

"Continuous or intermittent?" the chestnut haired, sienna eyed, olive skinned beauty asked.

"Continuous," Rocco said as he walked toward her. "How do you know about kilns?"

"Picked up a little information here and there. What type of work do you do?"

"My current project is a series of ceramic tiles for a mosaic installation at the gallery."

"The Fiancetti Gallery?" she asked with enthusiasm.

He nodded.

"It is a beautiful space. I just spent two hours there. Lorenzo Fiancetti is ..... well, you know how brilliant he is."

"How so?"

"You are working in his studio and you said you will be doing an instillation at his gallery. You must recognize his talent and he yours," she smiled.

Rocco studied the young woman. His attention unnerved her. "I apologize for staring, but you are quite exquisite. You are Greek, si?"

"I should be going. It's getting late. Good luck with your installation."

Before he could respond, the wonder was gone.

~

Rocco spent a few minutes at the closed Fiancetti Gallery surveying his completed pieces. The image was taking shape as the mosaics lined up and touched one another. The young artist was joined in the private room by his father, world renowned artist Lorenzo Fiancetti.

"It is quite beautiful, son. Was your day at the kiln successful?"

"Si. And you? Did you work at your studio?"

"No. I spent the day at the fountain at Piazza de Ferrari with my sketch pad. Perhaps tomorrow I will lock myself in the studio. How long before you are ready to install your piece?"

"Two days at the kiln three days to install. Do you think I made an error using only three colors?"

"That is a question only you can answer. It was a risk. A bold risk. You fear people will think I created it and question whether it is your work, si?"

Rocco nodded.

The father tapped his son's shoulder, "Go home. Get some rest. Finish your piece and let the world have their say. You are an artist, Rocco. The need to create will fuel you. Self-doubt will chase you. Welcome to the club."

~

Rocco left out the back door of the gallery, made his way to the studio to check the kiln, then moved down the brick alleyway toward his terraced apartment. As he passed a doorway, he found the exquisite wonder cowered tight in the small space, her knees pulled to her chest, her face pressed deep against them.

"What the hell do you think you're doing?" Rocco demanded.

Wonder began to rise, "I'm sorry. I'll find another place."

"You'll come with me."

She flinched – made a move to get around him.

"Don't even think about running. What's your name?"

"I'd rather not say."

"What do you want me to call you?"

"You pick," she said with a shrug.

Rocco scoffed, "You'll tell me when you're ready. I'm Rocco. Let's go."

"Where?"

"My place."

She stopped.

He stopped.

"I have a garden flat. I'll leave the terrace doors open, and will not try to stop you from leaving. You look as though you haven't eaten or rested in days."

Her exhale seemed to take with it the last bit of energy she had. The silent wonder didn't pull away when he took hold of her hand and led her into his garden place.

"Do you want food or a nap first?"

"Could I take a shower, please?"

"It's right through there. Whatever you need is in the closet in the bathroom or in the bedroom chest of drawers."

Twenty minutes later Wonder emerged with her hair wrapped in a towel and her face scrubbed clean. She had on a pair of jeans and one of Rocco's T-shirts, "I hope you don't mind. I needed to rinse my shirts and you said to take what I needed."

He eyed the exceedingly beautiful young woman, couldn't help but notice her round breasts and pebbled nipples, "My T-shirt never looked better."

She neither responded nor shied from his attention.

"I have reheated lasagna," the host said as he placed her plate on the table. He poured her a glass of wine then sat opposite her. "How long have you been on the streets?"

Wonder, with the sienna eyes, finished her mouthful and smiled, "It's not like that. I have a home – I prefer not to be in it."

"Is someone after you?"

She took another bite and nodded.

"Has someone hurt you?" Rocco watched her face, her beautiful face. Her eyes glistened with tears that held tight. "I think I should go. My things can dry outside, and I can return your shirt tomorrow." She pushed her chair back and got up.

He did the same. "I think you should stay the night. If you sit and finish your meal. I won't ask any questions."

Before she sat she unwrapped her hair, shook the long chestnut waves free, and pulled the front section to one side. She waited for Rocco to sit before she began eating again, "This is very delicious. Thank you for sharing."

"Thank you for staying, otherwise I would have to follow you throughout the labyrinth streets of Genoa. It would make for a very long night."

After waiting through Rocco's many, many minutes of reflection, Mick walks into the office and closes the door behind him, "March 5th."

"Mmm."

"Your son turns fifteen tomorrow. You should be with him."

"He'll want to know about his mother. He's becoming dogged with his questions."

Mick pauses then drops an envelope onto the desk that separates the two men.

"What's in the envelope, Mick?"

"Plane tickets. Go see Manuel."

"Is that an order, AIG Bentley?"

"If need be, Special Operative Duff."

We should talk.

The teen doesn't so much as flinch when he sees his father walking the length of hall outside the recording studio. He does, however, take a bit of pleasure when the man is refused entry by a red light over the door. The son holds his father in steady stare for several seconds, then returns his attention to the mixing board he's manipulating. The pissed young man remains inside the glass walled partition for two hours; leaving his father to stand outside. When the adolescent has had his fill of torturing his old man, he shuts down the board, removes a set of earphones, grabs his gear, kills the lights, and heads out. "You shouldn't have come," he says as he passes by.

"That's what I said, but Mick insisted."

Hearing Mick's name knocks Manuel back a bit. He stops and turns, "How is he?"

"Still feeling her loss. He and The Duff preceded you."

"I know."

"It's your birthday," the father smiles.

"I know."

"We should talk."

"Unless you're here to tell me about my mother, we have nothing to say."

Ashes to ashes.
Answers to questions.

Manuel Xavier, Alistair Duff, and Mick Bentley are at the Bentley Family Sheep Farm in Leicestershire, England, a landlocked county in the English Midlands. The reason for the get together is to mark the second anniversary of The Duff's passing and to witness the long-awaited scattering of Lady Frances' cremated remains. The men should be in somber reflection, but rather they are sharing a hearty laugh.

"This is where The Duff wanted to be rested – God only knows why, but she really loved it here," her lover of twenty years casually notes, "understatement forthwith, it was no easy fait accompli. Her certified request put a few royal knickers in a twist. Imagine the indignity of a royal – even this royal – being mucked about at a sheep farm. It was pure wickedness on The Duff's part."

Alistair takes great pleasure in Mick's telling, "Have to say, old man, I'm surprised the royal lot consented."

"Yes, well, Duff's request contained an addendum. Let's just say that had there been any rebuff of The Duff a salacious tidbit would have found its way into public domain, and a very royal-royal would be out on his duff straight away."

After another round of laughter, the men settle a bit for somber reflection. When he's had his fill, Mick shoulders the teary-eyed teen, "Come on kid, let's head to the farmhouse, I understand Alistair has things to discuss."

Mick sits across from Manuel and sets the topic of discussion. "Eleni."

"My mother."

"Yes."

"You knew her?"

"No, but I was there the day she delivered you."

Manuel addresses his father who has taken space against a wall across the room. "I searched the internet for her after you told me her name." He rolls his eyes Mick's way, "Her first name. That's it. That's all he got out before he walked away."

Mick nods.

Alistair edges in, "I saw your internet searches – they were for Eleni and Alistair."

Manuel nods.

"You needed to search for Eleni and Rocco."

Manuel facepalms, "Shit. I totally missed the mark."

"You wouldn't have found anything. What little there was about us has been scrubbed."

Alistair turns and looks out at the rolling farmland. "I'll tell you everything, Manuel, but after today you will no longer think of me as Alistair Duff. You will know me as Rocco Fiancetti, a clandestine operative of the SIS, former husband of Eleni Karras, and cold-blooded killer of Andros Karras."

Mick pushes in—**hard**, "You killed Karras in self-defense."

"That's your story, AIG Bentley."

"**And yours**," another hard push.

The father locks eyes with his son, "I avenged the murder of your mother."

"Shit. No wonder you scrubbed this from the internet."

Rocco nods and introduces another player into the mix. "Lorenzo Fiancetti is your grandfather."

"The artist."

"Si."

Manuel laughs, "Si? What the fuck is, si?"

Mick pushes in, "Alistair, is this really the time to introduce the kid to all aspects of Rocco Fiancetti?"

"Si."

Mick groans, "Okay, look Manuel. This may be a bit confusing. Try to follow along as best as you can and I'll help translate."

"Translate? Is he going to speak in Italian?" the kid stammers.

"Worse. He's going to speak in Rocco." Mick cautions the kid's father, "Filter it."

"Si. I, Rocco Fiancetti, am the production of a single liaison between the lady and the artist. There are — there were — five people who know my parentage: The Duff, your grandmother. Lorenzo, your grandfather. Cepriano Batista, your paternal great-uncle. Mick and Maverick. The Duff raised me in England, accompanied me on clandestine summerings with Lorenzo, and when emancipation was such, I lived as Rocco Fiancetti in Genoa. That is where I learned my craft from the master."

"Did you get all that, Manuel?" Mick asks with the shake of his head.

"Si," the kid jabs, "except the craft part."

Rocco looks out the window once again, and gets lost in thought…

Genoa, Italy
1989

Rocco woke to the smell of something wonderful. He followed his nose and stomach to the kitchen, watched as his visitor separated a very thick tomato and pepper sauce into wells into which she dropped an egg. When the eggs poached to perfection, she removed the cast iron skillet from the stove and addressed her guest.

"My name is Eleni Karras. I am the only child of Greek shipping tycoon, Andros Karras. Depending on your point of view I am on an unplanned holiday traveling across Europe or I have run away from my father's home on the island of Santorini. In return for your hospitality I have made Shakshuka for your morning meal. Fair warning, if my father's henchman, Nikos Galanos, finds me here with you, this will be your last meal. So enjoy your Shakshuka, Rocco Fiancetti."

The young man smiled and nodded, "I see that you've been doing more than cooking this morning, Eleni."

"I've done some snooping – just to level the playing field, Rocco. I found your name on several lavender envelopes, but I did not read the letters. They are from your lover, perhaps?"

"Perhaps." **Rocco took a bite of Shakshuka and moaned,** "quite good."

Eleni smiled, "I guessed you liked it when your taste buds moaned. After I have cleaned your kitchen, I will be on my way."

"Are you traveling alone? Completely alone?"

"But of course. It is customary that runaways embark on a solitary journey, si?" **she offered a smile.**

"Perhaps. But most runaways aren't as beautiful as you, Eleni. You are asking for trouble being on your own."

"Most of my days on Earth have included trouble, Rocco. I have just begun my travels, and have several more cities and many more galleries to find. If you don't want my travels to be lonely, come with," she tossed a playful smile his way.

Rocco said nothing for a few minutes. "I need five days to finish the installation at the gallery. If you stay here with me during that time, I will travel with you."

Eleni clapped her hands and ran to Rocco. She wrapped her arms around his neck and pecked him on his cheek. "We will have romance and adventure. A summer to remember."

"Eleni," Rocco whispers.

"Eleni," Manuel repeats. "Was my mother Greek?"

"Si."

"Was she beautiful?"

"Si. She was a wonder."

Missing curfews.

Maverick Cross is waiting at the far end of Stonesthrow bridge for Manuel to return from The Duff's 'scattering'. For the better part of the past two years, Maverick has had sole custody of and responsibility for Manuel Xavier. For most of that time the two have been traveling to Maverick's gigs, or living at The Music Farm.

Set on a 200-acre parcel of land a 'stone's throw' from Avon, Ohio, The Music Farm just happened one day in 1995. On September 2nd of that year, the Rock & Roll Hall of Fame held a concert at the Cleveland Municipal Stadium to celebrate the opening of its doors. Musicians, and fans of musicians from around the world flocked to be part of the momentous occasion and bear witness to the likes of James Brown, Bob Dylan, Jerry Lee Lewis, Aretha Franklin, and Johnny Cash – legends who rocked the hell out of Cleveland. For some reason—and there are countless stories as to what that reason was—performers and concertgoers made their way 15 miles west to the shore of Lake Erie where there was open farmland a 'stone's throw' and over a bridge from Avon. The vagabonds set up camp and staked their claim. Sounds of music – and the sweet smell of community –

filled the air, and before the week was over, a group of benefactors had purchased the land and incorporated it for the development of—

The Music Farm
Where musicians plant their seeds
and harvest their songs.

Seeding and harvesting at The Farm is seasonal, which means most artists stay for three months then move on. They arrive with the clothes on their back and little else. The Farm has every conceivable thing a musician, songwriter, or sound engineer could ever need to hone their craft. The 50, one-room cabins are booked solid with a waiting list of two years out. All costs are handled through a grant program, and visiting artists are selected by scouts who frequent high school dances, college campuses, and small venues looking for someone who might have 'rooting' potential.

Maverick Cross, a well-established, Grammy-winning musician, grabbed a gig as a scout when his best friend gave him a teenager to raise. The one for whom Maverick is waiting at Stonesthrow bridge.

"Aw shit," Maverick grunts when he sees Manuel dragging his ass toward the covered crossover. "Is this gonna be another moody month, Manuel?" he calls out. "You're worse than a menstruating woman."

A woman within earshot calls out, "Fuck you, Cross."

"No offense intended," he shouts back.

"Fuck you, anyway."

By the time Manuel steps off the bridge he's laughing. "No mood, just looping the shit through."

"Some shit."

"I heard you're one of the five people who knows the story of Eleni and Rocco."

He nods.

"Are you gonna fill in some of the gaps."

"Let's have some food and shit, then head to The Silo, there's a singer I want you to hear. Then we'll talk."

"Singer? Someone **you** scouted?"

"Yes."

"A female then," Manuel laughs. "People around here think you're a dog, you know."

"I know."

"So, who's the singer and what's her thing."

"Her name is Vivi, and she hasn't a clue what her thing is. She's good at everything: teen pop, post-grunge, contemporary pop-rock, alternative-indie rock, she does it all and she does it all really well. She's young so she's got time to find whatever IT is."

"What do you think she should do?"

"Whatever fills her."

What filled Vivi that night was a set of Melissa Etheridge, Janis Joplin, and Tracy Chapman covers.

"Shit," Manuel exhaled. "She should do **that**."

The 'she' in reference makes her way to Maverick's table. "You wanted to see me, Mr. Cross."

Maverick nods, "Vivi, this is Manuel Xavier."

"Hi, fair warning, I happen to be a menstruating woman, and I'm in a bitchin mood."

Manuel and Vivi bust out laughing.

"Oh for bloody sake," Maverick grunts.

That choice of words sets off a new round of laughter the teens take with them on the way out of The Silo, "Don't wait up Maverick," Manuel calls over his shoulder.

"The Farm's curfew is 1 AM. Don't break it."

A few quiet seconds pass, then... "Mr. Cross said you play piano," the cute girl with shorn blonde hair and chocolate-brown eyes says with a hip-chuck.

"A little."

"You don't get accepted at Mozart International unless you play the **hell** out of a piano."

"Mr. Cross could learn a few things from my father about keeping his mouth shut."

"Who's your father?"

"Haven't a clue. Where are we going?"

"Studio-12. I booked a couple of hours, figure you can play a 'little' piano, or do some sound mixing. If you're up to it, you know, jetlag and all."

"Damn. What else did he tell you?"

Vivi shrugs.

Two hours became three then four and by the time 1 AM rolled around the teens had an audience. Manuel banged the hell out of the keys and Vivi hit all the right notes. For the next three months, Vivi and Xavier made great music together — and that night, well, they missed curfew by a long shot.

Italy

Mick Bentley placed several calls to Rocco's cell phone after he dropped Manuel at London's Heathrow Airport. The calls went ignored. When he got back to his flat, he texted: **I suspect you're in Casella. Reach out when you're done.**

Rocco Fiancetti listened to Mick's message. Twice. The second time was just as the Thello arrived at the narrow-gauge railway station in the mountainous village of Casella. The anxious man bounds off the train, turns off his cell, tucks it into his pocket, and hoofs it toward a little stone cottage set on a beautiful bit of rocky terrain in the Liguria region of Italy. He's only just arrived at the twin entrance pillars when memories of his time with Eleni erupt from wherever he's tried to bury them…

Genoa, Italy
1989

Rocco implored Eleni to stay at his terraced place while he worked in the heat studio.

"Stay inside where you are safe. It is the only way I can concentrate on my work. We can talk when I get back. Please wait here." he said as he rushed out.

Eleni stayed inside, for the most part, although she ventured along the brick alleyway from time to time to catch a glimpse of the young artist at work. On one such trip, her movements were watched by a man tucked into the doorway that offered her respite the night before. The man waited until she returned from her spying, then approached. Eleni gasped, first out of fear, then again when she recognized the man.

"I didn't disturb your son's work, Mr. Fiancetti," she offered a preemptive defense.

"I am quite sure you would have if he'd seen you — you are quite lovely ..... I'm sorry, but I do not know your name."

Rocco's guest smiled, "Eleni, my name is Eleni."

Rocco's father bent at the waist, "I am Lorenzo."

Eleni's smile widened, "Yes. The most celebrated contemporary artist known the world over for his tri-color paintings."

Lorenzo nodded and smiled.

Eleni recognized the wide, dimpled smile as his son's. "I am a fan, Mr. Fiancetti. I spent several hours at your gallery yesterday."

"Ah, the beautiful girl — my gallery assistant mentioned you. Please Eleni tell me why you are a fan of my work."

"That will take some time. May we talk at Rocco's place?"

"Please, after you." Lorenzo waited at the terrace door while Eleni poured two glasses of wine. He noticed the bedding on the couch and a small backpack placed by the front door. Noticed, too, how the young woman looked over her shoulder and checked the faces of those who passed by. The artist and his fan took seats on the terrace and enjoyed some of their wine before Eleni began.

"I am a lover of your tri-color pieces. Three colors on a canvass. Think about that for a minute. Of all the colors in the universe what would compel an artist to limit himself to three colors? Had I not seen your work, and only had someone tell me there is a fascination in three colors on a canvass I would not have believed it." Eleni took a quick sip of her wine before continuing, "The thing is, I don't see three colors. Oh, initially I do, I mean if there's red, green and yellow then that is what I see. But the longer I look at a piece the intensity of the three colors fade and in their place I see an abundance of colors, subtle as they may be." The young art enthusiast appreciated the look of interest on the artist's face – it encouraged her on. "For instance, one of the colors you used in your piece, Meadow Days, was lemon-yellow. Within minutes of staring at the bright citrusy, mouth-watering yellow," she snapped her fingers, "the lemon is gone and is replaced with the warmth of butter, or the lift of goldenrod, or the jaundice of the sickly. I don't know how it happens, but it is remarkable." Eleni blushed when she realized the

length of her gushing. "I'm sorry, I haven't let you have a word, or maybe my rambling has rendered you speechless."

"Eleni, I haven't been in the company of anyone who knows my work as well as you do. This has been the most wonderful time. Now, tell me about you and my son, who I believe is nearby eavesdropping."

When Rocco stepped near, it was Eleni's turn to be rendered speechless.

~

The evening of the private unveiling of Rocco's mosaic began with excitement and ended with enticement.

"It is exquisite Rocco," **Eleni said for the umpteenth time.**

Rocco swelled with pride, "I have been questioning the choice of three colors."

Eleni's eyes do not leave his work, "Because of your father's success with tri-color work?"

"Si."

Eleni took hold of the young artist's hand, "This work is uniquely your own, Rocco. I think it is bold to enter his world and find your own place within. I fancy myself a devotee of your father's work so believe me when I say that this piece will usher you toward your own place in the art world."

"Eleni is correct, son," **Lorenzo spoke from behind them.** "This work is a triumph. The choice of blue, brown, and white, and the placement of the tiles is perfection. The final piece demands attention. The power, the serenity, the wonder it's all there."

"It's Santorini," Eleni whispered.

"What?"

"The mosaic. It's Santorini. The colors are of my homeland. The brown represents the carved out, assaulted terrain left behind after one of Earth's most powerful volcanic eruptions ever to be recorded. The white swaths across the top of the earth tones represents the whitewash houses perched precariously over a land destined to roar again. And the blues of the sky and the sea share a clandestine kiss on the horizon — that locks the story of Santorini."

Rocco released Eleni's hand and placed his on either side of her face. He ran his thumbs over every inch of her beauty then pulled her in for a claiming kiss. His desire captured every bit of air from the room. The soon-to-be-lovers barely heard the closing of the door behind Lorenzo.

"Eleni." Rocco touched and kissed the wonder who walked into his life only days before. He had yet to enter her, but her silk was already home to him. He celebrated her beauty with feather soft kisses and owning touches as he stripped her bare. His response was fierce, his touch, reverent. "Exquisite. You are a work of art."

Eleni pressed herself tight against him, touched his face and with shaking hands began undressing him. Her moves were halting, her breathing hitched with desire — uncertainty.

Rocco shared his nakedness, his want powerfully displayed.

Eleni raised a hand to her cheek to conceal the blush that took hold.

Rocco feared the signs, "Eleni, am I the first?"

Tears stung her eyes, "Yes."

He stepped back.

She closed the space between them. "Rocco, I have never given myself to anyone. I have never desired this. I have never trusted anyone. Please let me have this with you beneath your beautiful masterpiece." Silent tears fell from beneath closed lashes as she felt him walk away. Her pain and embarrassment began to settle, yet she was unable to move – unable to cover her naked pain.

A touch on her arms startled her. "Come, Eleni." Rocco directed her to the bed he'd made of their clothes and set beneath his mosaic. They lay together, touching, kissing, offering themselves. He waited until she was ready – his probing was gentle, her response unbridled. When she begged him to enter her – He begged her to never leave.

Eleni's release was quick and steady.

Rocco's was halted. He abruptly pulled himself free – moaned against her as he finished, "Eleni. Eleni." He looked at the beauty beneath him. "Eleni, look at me."

Her focus was fleeting, her smile, telling. "Rocco. Such wonders of life. Thank you." She reached to touch his face.

He took her hand and kissed its palm. "Eleni, are you on the pill or anything?"

The young woman who had part of her lover pooled within pushed from beneath him. "I have to go," she said on a panic.

"Go? You aren't going anywhere, Eleni." He tried to pull her to him.

She pushed angrily away. "I have to go, Rocco. He will kill you if he learns of this." Her panic swelled as she hurriedly donned her clothes.

Rocco responded in kind pushing his legs into his jeans. "Eleni, tell me what is going on. Are you having regrets about us?"

Eleni shook her head, "No regrets of us. But I have put you in danger. I am the daughter of a ruthless man. He does not see me as your father sees you, Rocco. To Andros Karras I am a possession. His prized possession. If he learns that you have defiled and perhaps impregnated his prized possession, he will destroy you."

Rocco pulled his wonder to him. "If another man tries to take you away, I will destroy him."

~

Rocco and Eleni left Genoa and married the day they learned she was pregnant. They traveled the Mediterranean coastline, spending time in Portofino, Porto Venere, Venazza and Rapallo, and when Eleni tired and needed to settle for the last months of her pregnancy, they headed to Casella at the urging of Lorenzo.

"Settle at the stone cottage of your uncle. Share your first Christmas, welcome your baby after the New Year, then return to Genoa. Andros Karras can try to rip his daughter from a lover's arms, but he cannot take a wife from her husband or a mother from her child."

The weary travelers made their way to the mountainous village of Casella northeast of Genoa arriving days before Christmas. They kept to themselves, she nesting, he sketching, and traveling into the village only when they needed provisions. Over time Rocco friended the local grocer, Tomas, and his wife Maria. A week before Eleni's due date, Rocco invited them to his home.

"Your wife is very along. She will deliver here, Rocco?" Tomas asked.
"Si."
"You have experience?"
"No."
"Do not worry, Maria is one of seven and has participated in many births. She will help. Si, Maria?"
"Si. We will all help Eleni to motherhood."

After laboring for more than a day, Eleni Karras Fiancetti delivered her son in a stone cottage in Casella, Italy. Before sunrise the next day, Eleni was gone…

London, England
1990

Rocco Fiancetti, known in the U.K. as Alistair Duff found himself in a most unenviable place — sitting in the same room with both of his parents. If not for the circumstances of the moment he would consider this the most interesting day of his life.

His mother, Frances Duff, whose lineage traced back to the 1st Duke of Fife teetered on the edge of an antique chair. The regal woman of 42, with ramrod posture and put-upon attitude, looked positively agonized. This surprised Alistair not in the least given the woman was in the company of the man who caused her public humiliation and royal banishment. Nor did it surprise him that his father was seconds away from poking the lady.

"You're looking good, Franny."

"Pig."

"Shrew."

Rocco smirked, "Well this is interesting, but if it's all the same to you two children, I'm in a serious situation and you aren't helping."

"He started it," Frances motioned with her head.

Lorenzo leaned toward her and stared at her face.

"What on earth are you doing, Lorenzo?"

"Checking for a nosebleed, Franny."

"Miscreant."

"Aristocrat."

"Artist."

"Elitist."

Mick Bentley stormed into the conference room at the MI6 Headquarters, "The whole floor has stopped working on matters of National concern to listen to the two of you swipe at one another. Attention appreciated. I've been listening to this crap for far too many years."

Alistair turned bewildered eyes toward the SIS operative, "You are aware that Frances Duff is of royal lineage?"

Mick laughed, "I am aware that I drew the short straw and am forced to work with these two. If The Duff wants to dismiss me, bloody hell, if she wants me run through with a saber on palace property, I won't object."

The Fiancetti men noticed the look, the smile, and the wink between the Operative and The Duff.

Lorenzo **could not** let that moment pass, "A tad on the young side, Franny."

"Cad."

"Scrubber."

The room pulled quiet.

The look on Frances Duff's face at being referred to as a woman of low social standing was a blow too closely aligned with her insecurities.

Alistair and Mick threw death-stares at Lorenzo. He missed them all as he was moving toward the woman he'd hurt. "Frances, my apologies."

She slapped his face, then offered him the tiniest smile, "We do bring out the worst in one another, Lorenzo."

He tilted his head to their son, "And the best."

Mick and Alistair shook their heads and took their seats at the conference table. Frances and Lorenzo joined them.

Mick began the meeting, "Eleni is back in Santorini or more precisely she is being held on one of her father's yachts in the South Aegean Sea off the island's coast. Nikos Galanos, Andros Karras' right-hand-man is her guard and is with her 24-7. We have an operative on the waitstaff who has orders to intervene only if Eleni is threatened in any way. She is completely unaware of this person's duplicity. I have others in the area who report that whenever the yacht moves close to land Eleni moves to the main deck. We think she is hopeful someone will recognize her and will report back to you, Alistair. Technically, that is what is happening at this meeting."

The conference room grew quiet – the only sounds came from the bundle wrapped tightly in the young father's arms. "Will there be a rescue attempt?" he asked.

"We have no authority in Santorini, certainly none on the yacht of Andros Karras."

"Then why do you have an operative with her?" Rocco pushed.

"For her protection. And should a day come when Andros Karras gets in our crosshairs, we will be ready to act."

Frances Duff addressed Mick Bentley, "How can I help?"

Alistair stood and answered the question by placing Manuel into his mother's arms, "You can raise my son."

After three days in Casella, reliving his life with Eleni, and mourning her loss, Rocco walks away from the stone cottage, steps onto the Thello, and places a call to Mick.

"I'm done."

2006

Manuel Xavier knows his father is lurking nearby. The music student has been in and out of the Meredith Wilson residence hall and the Juilliard school building five times. On each of his ins and outs, he's sensed the spy's presence. Manuel grabs his vibrating cell from his pocket. He expects to find a text from his father, he finds one from her: **At Lenny's.** He returns his cell to his pocket, changes course, and heads to Leonard Bernstein Way at West 65th and Broadway. He gives a little shout out to the spy he's sure is following him. "Come on, Rocco, we're going to see Vivi!" Manuel trenches a wide smile knowing he bested the clandestine spy.

The young man picks up his pace, eager to get to Lenny's – it's sort of become their place. The talented singer with shorn blonde hair and chocolate-brown eyes never told the talented pianist why they always meet at Lenny's, but Manuel knows – well, he knows part of it, anyway. As a student at Juilliard, Manuel is allowed to cross-register at Barnard College and Columbia University, so he's loaded up on computer classes at one campus, and economics at the other. He used his computer skills to do some cyber snooping on Vivi Faulkner. He learned she is a distant-distant-distant relative of the great, Leonard Bernstein. Vivi doesn't know that Manuel has made the connection, but he suspects the spy who's on his tail, the one who was recently promoted to the rank of Senior Special Operative, knows everything about his son and the girl who's in and out of his life.

Manuel puts his arm around the shivering young woman and plants a quick kiss, "Let's get some coffee." They step into their favorite spot, climb a few stairs to a loft area that has wall to wall book shelves surrounding well-worn club chairs and scuffed up end tables. They slide onto a corner bench, put their cups onto the table in front of them and try to rub some feeling back into Vivi's frigid fingers.

"Shit, it's cold."

"Where've you been?"

"Florida. I did a two week thing in Orlando. Sort of a trial run for spring break. I'll find out next week if I get the gig. If it's a go, I'll spend Christmas in New York, then head south. If not, I guess I'll spend Christmas in New York, and then wing it."

"If things don't work out, you can crash at The Music Farm."

"You're heading back?"

"For winter break. Maverick just started a three month stay, so I'm gonna spend the holidays with him and come back here at the end of January."

"He's in the studio?"

Manuel nods, smiles, then sips his coffee. "He's laying tracks."

"What's with the smile?"

"I'm playing on two of them, *Rain Down* and *Reno*."

Vivi nods, smiles, then sips her coffee. "It's about time."

"Yeah." He takes his eyes off the girl for a split second and sees his father wave to him from across the street. The son places his cup onto the table and grabs his jacket, "I'll be right back." By the time he gets outside, Alistair Duff aka Rocco Fiancetti is gone.

Mayflower, Massachusetts

Special Agent, John Maxwell, shuts down his FICA computer systems when his security camera hones in on a man walking toward the barn. He uses an access door that leads from his spy lair, to Netti Barn, his software design company and waits. After a minute or so, he steps outside, a gun firmly in hand.

The visitor is casually leaning against the side of the two-story, pale yellow structure. "You can put your gun away, Special Agent Maxwell."

John raises his gun, "Get the fuck inside."

The unwelcome visitor moves past the armed man and steps the fuck inside. "Now what?" he asks over his shoulder.

"Put your hands on your head. You have one minute to explain yourself."

"I should be asking you to explain the hole in your defense system. Very sloppy work, Special Agent Maxwell."

"Who the fuck are you?"

The man with his hands on his head laughs, "I'm MI6, but I doubt you'll accept that as fact." After many seconds of silence the man gives more, "Ah, you're entertaining the possibility that I am with U.K. cyber intelligence, after all, who else would know Sam Sawyer and John Maxwell are one and the same, and who else could penetrate your defense systems?" The man turns and lowers his hands, "Senior Special Operative, Alistair Duff, at your service."

"What the fuck hole did you find?"

"The one that led me here. When this story is told, AND this story will be told one day, remember that it was Alistair Duff who broke through the impenetrable defense system of the preeminent cyber defender."

John raises his gun, "Sit down."

"Special Agent Maxwell put your damn gun away. We both know you aren't going to kill an operative who works for your country's greatest ally."

"Don't fucking count on it."

"I'm here to tell you that you are susceptible. That your sloppiness has left your country vulnerable – not to mention FICA's Dead On Assignment agent."

John lowers his weapon.

Alistair takes a swipe. "Ah, I see DOA's vulnerability has hit a chord." The Operative walks past the Special Agent. "Fix the problem or I'll be back."

Sage Finley

2003

"Your daughter was attacked."

"What?"

"Some bastard got…"

The mother races past the bearer of bad news and out the door of The Mart, the lone convenience store located near Tucks, a low-income housing project in San Antonio, Texas.

"Some bastard got Sage. Busted her up bad, Sandra."

"Some bastard got Sage. Busted her up bad, Sandra."

"Some bastard got Sage. Busted her up bad, Sandra."

The words have looped through Sandra Finley's head plenty by the time she pushes into Unit 11 and calls out to her daughter, "Sage!"

The girl's response is lost to a whimper.

The mother moves quickly through the kitchen, tripping on a raised edge of linoleum that she's tripped on a hundred times before. Two steps later she is through the living room that doubles as her bedroom and is pushing open the door to her daughter's 6x6 foot room.

The sight of her bloody and bruised 15-year-old girl curled atop a threadbare spread pushes the last bit of air from the mother and pulls a pitiful moan from deep within. "Sage. Who? Ohhh, Sage." The mother sits on the corner of the pancake-thin mattress, and opens her arms to the daughter who would enter them if she could. After many minutes of stroking Sage's back, Sandra kicks off her shoes and eases onto the makeshift bed. She gently spoons her daughter until the wee hours.

"Momma."

"Mmmmm."

"Tell me again why I shouldn't make men pay for it."

Sandra is up early and waiting at the Friends Free Health Clinic when it opens its doors. A lovely, petite blonde medical aide ushers her in, "I heard about Sage."

The mother breaks at those words, finds the first chair and drops herself onto it. Many minutes pass before she's able to conduct her business, "The Morning After Pill, can I get it, please."

"I already put it aside, and some other things – pamphlets, medical supplies, and whatnot. I was going to drop them off this morning. Sage should come in for an exam."

"She will." The rail-thin mother in clothes that'd seen better days – countless days ago –

musters the last of her resolve. "Do you … have you … do you know who…?"

The medical aide nods, "I can't repeat what I've heard, Ms. Finley, but it's common knowledge on the streets. I'm sure if you ask along the route home, you'll get his name."

Sandra Finley gets his name – from every woman she meets along her way home. By the time she's back at #11, the mother has a fire lit deep within. She pushes into the kitchen full of rage then loses it when she finds her 15-year-old daughter nursing a cup of tea around a busted and bruised bottom lip. The mother puts the bag of medical supplies onto the table, hands her daughter a pill packet, gets a glass of water and instructs, "Take it.

"Will it keep me from getting pregnant?"

"Yes."

"You were my age when you got pregnant."

"Yes."

"Shit, Momma."

"Take the pill, Sage." Sandra filled the saucepan with water and waits for it to boil then joins Sage at the table, "You should go get checked out at the clinic."

"I will."

"Today."

"Okay."

"Do you want me to go with…"

"No."

After many quiet minutes, Sandra speaks – very softly. "Sage, I know who…"

The 15-year-old rape victim lashes out, "Momma! It doesn't matter who it was. This one got angry and rough, but you already know that the boys at Tucks have been helping themselves to me since I got these," she stops and points to her breasts. The teen pulls a ragged breath and continues, "So now that you know who, what's your plan? We have him arrested? The cops mess with him a bit. He gets out and pays me back for his troubles by doing a whole lot worse the next time."

Sandra Finley stares at her daughter, pitifully offering nothing.

"Exactly Momma, we should keep our mouths shut," she turns to leave, turns back and finishes her say, "I should get a pimp and charge for use of my pussy — then maybe I wouldn't have to live in this shithole!" The damaged girl storms out the front door and doesn't come back until midnight. She finds her momma sitting in the dark on the busted-up kitchen floor. She takes a seat nearby and puts her head onto her mother's lap.

"I'm sorry, Momma."

"You're not the one who should be sorry, Sage."

2005

A cab pulls to the curb in front of Unit 11 in the most dangerous housing project in San Antonio. As a rule, cabs do not frequent Tucks. The cabbie would have let his fare off on the thoroughfare, but he couldn't see his way to. "Do you need help getting to your door?"

Sandra Finley shakes her head and gets out. She hasn't made it five steps when she collapses.

Sage wasn't home to witness the event, but she heard about it as she made her way through the projects just before dark. She eventually stops listening about the event and runs the rest of the way home. She pushes through the front door, and breathlessly calls out, "Momma!"

"In here, Sage."

"Momma. You collapsed? You were in a cab? Momma."

"Sage, calm down. I'm fine now."

A push of memories finds the daughter…

"Momma, do you have the flu?"

"Got something, that's for sure. You should keep your distance."

"Are you going to The Mart?"

"Don't think I can."

"Do you want me to take your shift?"

Sandra Finley nodded her head and rushed off to the bathroom.

~

Sage entered #11 and was greeted by the sounds of dry heave retching. "Momma," she called as she knocked on the bathroom door. "Can I come in? Do you need help? Are you sick again?"

"I need one of those drinks that help balance your blood, or whatever, and some square salt crackers."

"On it." Sage grabbed three dollars from a red sneaker tucked in the back of her closet and ran to The Mart. When she returned, she found her momma sitting in her beat-up recliner in the living room looking better than Sage expected based on the previous retch fest. "Here, I got you the cherry one."

"My favorite. Thank you."

Sandra quietly waits while her daughter pulls at the last few threads. She can tell from the changing facial expressions on her teen's face that Sage's thoughts are taking her toward the reality of things – and when the girl's tears spring forth she knows Sage has arrived at the end of her mother's story.

"Momma?" the young woman whispers as she takes hold of her mother's hand.

The ill woman offers a weak smile. "We should talk."

2006

Sage Finley walks out of Kale Friends High School on the last day of junior year. Her last year. The just-turned eighteen-year-old has resigned herself to being a high school dropout, and that she'll be taking over her mother's job at The Mart fulltime, and she'll never get out of Tucks — but what she hasn't yet accepted is the painful truth that she's losing her momma. On her way home, Sage stops by Friends Free Health Clinic, even though she'd already been by twice that week. The anxious daughter of a cancer patient can tell what the woman behind the Plexiglas window is going to say, but she asks her question anyway. "Has Momma been accepted into a clinical trial?"

Marcy shakes her head, "But we're sending in another round of applications in a few days. Your momma is at the top of the list." The medical aide raises a finger, "Hang on."

Sage studies the woman as she flits about. She figures Marcy and her momma are probably the same age, even though Marcy looks a decade younger. Sage reflects on a whisper. "Living at Tucks makes you old and makes you dead, before your time." She continues watching the petite blonde rummage through a few wire bins for some supplies, grab hold of a brown paper bag, shove the stuff in, and walk it to the doorway. "There's some anti-nausea medicine, some drinks that will balance your momma's electrolytes, and some others for nourishment. And I can't give anything for pain other than OTCs, but the ones I put in are the strongest we have."

"Thank you, Marcy."

Sage is two blocks from #11, when HE slows his ride and creeps along beside her.

"Get in bitch."

Sage shifts the weight of the heavy bag, ignores his call, and picks up her pace a bit.

"You deaf, bitch?"

Sage shifts the weight of the heavy bag, ignores his call, and picks up her pace a bit more.

"You make me get out of this car, I'll beat your ass, then fuck you raw."

Sage stops dead in her tracks – places the heavy bag onto the busted up sidewalk – stomps to the car – and calls out, "Darrell Hawks! This Darrell Hawks," she points to the car, "raped me when I was fifteen!"

"Shut the fuck up bitch!"

The commotion between the two pulls a dozen or so people from their places. Sage Finley uses the audience and the rest of her moxie, "I am declining Darrell Hawks' order to get into his car. I am picking up my bag. I am walking home. Where I will tend to my dying mother." She turns and does exactly as she said she'd do.

And her rapist – well he creeps right along behind her.

When Sage gets to #11, Darrell Hawks toots and shouts, "I'll be back when your momma's dead, and when I get done with you, you're gonna wish you were dead."

The Emporium

Eve Lappier, owner of the dating service destined to close its doors by the end of the summer, is shooting the shit with some of her clients. This particular group of women do not come to The Emporium because they're looking for love, they're more interested in the wining and dining of dating. They pony up the $50 monthly dating fee, and in return they get a whole bunch of dates with a whole bunch of guys who spend a whole bunch of money on the wining and the dining of dating. Eve knows the women are giving a little something-something in return for the men's hospitality, but she keeps her nose out of that end of their business.

Sherry Santana, a beautiful henna haired, blue eyed regular hands Eve a piece of paper upon which she's written the heading—

Garden of Eve

"What's this?"

"The name of your new business."

Eve slides the paper back across the counter, "Damn, Sherry, it's gonna take me a million years to pay off the loan on this place. There's no way…"

"You don't need a new loan and Garden of Eve isn't a completely new business, it's a revamped version of The Emporium."

"Yeah, heavy on the word vamp," Deena Sutton giggles then adds, "Madam Eve."

Purely for shits and giggles Eve Lappier plays along. "So you five women want me to turn my dating service into a brothel."

"Yes, Madam Eve," they singsong.

"We've sort of worked a few things out for you," Sherry offers. "Here," she hands Eve a pen, "we'll talk, you write."

Eve jots a few notes as the girls toss a few ideas. An hour later, the girls leave, Eve closes the front door of The Emporium, and places an order for a new business sign.

The Mart

Sage's heart skips a beat when she sees Marcy step out of a little SUV, enter the convenience store, walk to the counter, put an envelope upon it, smile wide, and walk out. Sage offers a wide, toothy smile Heavenly knowing that for the very first time in her life, her prayers have been answered. She wants to tear into that envelope, but she wants her momma to have the joy of learning she's been accepted into a clinical trial. For the next two hours and seventeen minutes, Sage checks the clock a total of 137 times. As soon as her replacement arrives, she bolts out the door, runs as fast as she can, ignores the stitch in her side, and the ragged pull of air. She pushes into #11 calling out, "Momma! Momma! You're in!"

Sandra drags herself off the bathroom floor and to her recliner, "The trial? I'm in the trial?"

Sage holds the envelope out, "Marcy brought this to The Mart. I'm sure that's what it says, go on Momma open it."

Sandra reaches a shaky hand then pulls it back, "You read it."

Sage's eyes fill. She pulls the paper to her chest and hugs it close, "You're in, Momma."

Sandra's eyes fill because the dying woman knows it's already too late.

Malcolm Price

2003

The recent college graduate sits on the front stoop of his Mama Girl's row house at 11-B Cross Street in Lewisburg, Pennsylvania. The Burg, a rather cute name given to the blighted area, isn't one of those places where people tend to sit and enjoy a June evening outdoor, but the hopeful NBA draft pick is finding the quarters inside a bit too tight. From the kitchen, sounds of clinking and clanking dishes being washed, dried, and put away are a sure sign that his Mama Girl is feeling her own bit of angst. From the front room of the house, the steady drone of talking heads is annoying the young man deep to his bones, but he listens. After all, one of those two sports announcers will eventually call his name and that of the team he'll be playing for.

"Sit tight players. This is gonna be a l.o.n.g. night."

"Right you are, Don. The 2003 NBA draft roster might just have the most talented pool in draft history. We already know that the first selection this evening will go to Cleveland. Chairman, Gordon Gund, announced in May that the Cavs will pick LeBron James, so there'll be no surprise there. The

second and third selections will go to the Detroit Pistons and the Denver Nuggets and there's lots of speculation about who they will pull, then..."

"...then it will get really interesting and I suspect frustrating for the players. And these PLAYERS – any one of them could have been the first round pick: Marquette's, Dwayne Wade, and Georgia Tech's, Chris Bosh, and Georgetown's, Michael Sweetney, and Bucknell's, Malcolm Price, and Xavier's, David West, and—

Malcolm tosses the rock he's been flipping from hand to hand, watches it skip across the street and drop through a sewer grate. He gets up from the stoop, climbs four concrete stairs, and presses his back tight against the wall by the screen door. With each player's name called, his head hangs a little lower and his hands clench a little tighter.

"And the number ten slot goes to..."
"And the number twenty slot goes to..."
"And it looks like Malcolm Price is headed to..."

Alamo Heights
"Welcome to San Antonio, Mr. Price." JJ Packard raises his hand and smiles wide, "Give me a minute, I need to text my bookie and place a standing bet on the Spurs. With you pounding their parquet they ought to be bringing home another championship or two in right order."

59

Malcolm smiles wide, "No pressure though," his smile widens.

"None intended. You already made bank, Mr. Price. A cool fifty-five-mill spread out over three years, last I heard."

"Malcolm smiles and nods.

"My advice .... though you haven't asked for it, it's free of charge."

Malcolm smiles and nods.

"Buy a place, pound the boards, and enjoy the game."

"That's the plan, JJ." The young player walks a bit, takes some wall space, presses his back tight, and crosses his feet at his ankles. Tell me about the place."

"The top floor of the Haskin building has two condo units each with 2,000 square feet of living space. As you can see, the 16x17 foot living room has corner to corner, floor to ceiling windows that overlook downtown San Antonio. That section of windows right there opens outward to allow access to a balcony that wraps around the corner and has a similar opening into the partially walled 12x12 foot kitchen and 12x14 foot dining room. The kitchen is all stainless with white marble countertops, white custom cabinets, wine cooler and subzero refrigerator. On the opposite side is a 13x15 master with a 7x16 en suite master bath, and…"

"JJ. Let's just walk it."

Wyldwood, Texas

A young woman with long, crinkled, blonde hair and golden-brown eyes bangs her leg as she stands up at her desk. "Mr. Price? Did you have an appointment with Belinda?" she spins her head toward the appointment secretary who shrugs her shoulder.

"You recognize me?"

"Sure. The Spurs are **big** – even out here in Bastrop County. I hear you're wearing team jersey 77. Double numbers are lucky, you know."

"Didn't know ……….. " there's a fill in the blank pause.

She fills in the blank, "Sammi Wilcox." She smiles and offers another pause. "Ah. Since you don't have an appointment, would you like me to schedule some time with…"

"I'd like to see the McCaid place."

"Today?"

"Now."

"That's Belinda Donohue's listing, Mr. Price."

"Is Belinda here?"

"No. I suspect she's in the final stages of labor right about now."

"Then you should take me. I'm up from San Antonio and I'd like to buy the place."

"Now?"

"I'd like to see it first," he smiles.

Sammi throws it all to the wind, grabs her stuff, calls Chet McCaid, and takes Malcolm Price to the ranch. On the way, she tells him what she knows about Wyldwood Ranch – she knows a lot. "The 400+ acre ranch is located off the main thoroughfare in Wyldwood and has gated access to paved roads that lead to the frontend of the property. That's where the 5 bedroom rock and wood home with 4 car garage, nearby converted bunkhouse, and six horse stable with office and tack room are located. The back three-quarters of land is separated by a rock-bottom, cold water, spring fed river, and accessed only by a split-log bridge. The backend working acreage is fenced, has a bunkhouse for the live-on ranch hands, a 12-horse stable, three working barns and a two-story grain silo."

When Belinda Donohue phones in to the real estate office to announce the birth of her baby and learns that Sammi Wilcox is doing a frontend walkthrough of a multimillion-dollar property, she checks herself out of the hospital and hightails it to Wyldwood. She does her best to push the young realtor aside—only to learn that that's more difficult than pushing a nine-pound boy through a ten-centimeter opening.

"Thank you for coming, Ms. Donohue, but I'm working with Ms. Wilcox," Malcolm says with finality.

Sammi catches **the look** from her boss as she shuffles off toward her car. "Pretty sure my ass is fired for this," she whispers to the megabucks client.

"I'm buying the McCaid place from you Sammi. You'll make enough in commission that you won't need to work for Ms. Donohue." Malcolm pulls a business card from his pocket and hands it off.

Sammi reads it, "JJ Real Estate, San Antonio. Let me guess, there's a job offer waiting on me?" she laughs.

"No. There's a condo in Alamo Heights near the Center. JJ Packard is handling the listing. I want you working on it with him and split the commission. Sammi—I want **that** purchase to be **very** public. I don't want anyone knowing I'm buying the McCaid place out here in Wyldwood, not even JJ. This is how I'd like the purchases to be handled. I have a holding company, Lewis Burg LLC. The sales should go through—"

2005

Welcome to the 2005
NBA Championship Series
Western Conference – First Round

"For the second time in two years, the Spurs are in play for an NBA Championship title..."

"...and the man who'll be leading the charge again this year is Malcolm Price wearing team jersey 77. The Spurs newest point guard grew up in Lewisburg, Pennsylvania, attended Bucknell University where he played NCAA Division I ball in the Patriot League for four years. At 6'5" number 77 makes his presence on the boards known, and his exceptional ball handling and ability to read the court usually means he gets the job done..."

"...the nearly 20,000 fans packed into the SBC Center in San Antonio sure hope he gets the job done tonight..."

The twenty-three-year old **does not**
get the job done.

Alamo Heights
Malcolm Price is sitting alone on the balcony of his condo looking out at the skyline of San Antonio. The temp has dropped considerably and the man who's wearing nothing more than a pair of sweats should be feeling the cold—the man isn't feeling much of anything. The losing

player dragged his ass home more than an hour ago and hasn't moved a muscle since he parked that ass on a lounge chair. He hasn't had a conscious thought either, though every damn second from that night's game is on a torturous loop in his head. A slight disturbance from behind snaps him to. He calls over his shoulder when he hears the click of the front door, "Not in the mood for company, Jason."

"It's customary to welcome your guests in before you ask them to leave. You are in Texas, you know."

"After tonight's play, I doubt I'll be here long."

Jason Carpenter, head of Malcolm's ranch in Wyldwood, grabs a beer from the fridge and a seat on the balcony. "Damn, that sure was something awful to watch."

Malcolm laughs big.

"Spurs fans are packed in tight for Game 2 of First Round play in the Western Conference. By the end of tonight, Malcolm Price will have proved one of two things: he was the right draft pick two years ago, or..."

"...whoa...whoa...it's way too early to call this player's career. The whole team dropped the ball in fourth quarter play the other night. Twelve combined points is not gonna get you a win in Championship play..."

"...yeah, but 77 only put up 6 points during the whole game, and after ending his playoff-season

last year with a fractured thumb, you can't help but think maybe…"

77 thumbs his nose at the critics
by putting up 18 points and getting the job
done.

Alamo Heights
"This a thing now, Jason?"
"I was in the neighborhood."
"You were at the Center."
"Yeah. Figured I should be close by so as to drag your ass from the ledge of this balcony if you shit the boards again."
"Good call. You staying for a beer?"
"Nope. I'm heading back to the ranch, but I thought I'd drop this by."
Malcolm gives a quick look, "What's that?"
"San Antonio Express early edition."
"Am I keeping my job?"
"You decide," Jason tries to hand it off.
"Read it."
"The point guard scored some needed points in Game 2, and excelled in every other aspect at center court. Price ran the team's offense, handled the hell out of the ball, read the opposing team's defense, and got the ball to the Spurs player who could get the points — when he wasn't putting them up himself. Malcolm Price for the score and the win."

"Looks like I'll be heading to Denver for the next game," Malcolm smiles w.i.d.e.

Welcome to the 2005
NBA Championship Series
Western Conference – Semifinals

"It's Game 3 of the Semifinals and the Spurs are up two games coming into tonight's play at Key Arena in beautiful Seattle, Washington. Spurs number 77 has dominated play and has led his team to back to back wins with solid 20 point leads over the Sonics..."

"...but Price has gone from scoring a high of 26 points in the first game to a low of 6 in Game 2..."

"...but he's getting the job done..."

"...at home, but let's see if he can do IT on the road..."

Malcolm Price doesn't come anywhere
near to doing IT.

"Well, San Antonio, your team is back from Seattle and it's tied with the Sonics at 2 games each. That one point loss in Game 3 was a heartbreaker..."

"...but that humiliating 22 point loss in Game 4 begs the question..."

"...does 77 have what it takes to lead his team to a Championship title..."

"...let's not get ahead of ourselves. The question for today is whether Price can fix IT and bring IT tonight..."

The answer to both of those questions is a resounding, "Yes!"

Welcome to the 2005
NBA Championship Series
Conference – Finals

"It's Game 4 of the Conference Finals and the Spurs are up 3 games over the Phoenix Suns..."

"...77 and his team have LIT UP THE COURT! The Malcolm Price scored 15, 22, and 29 points in the first three outings, and with another showing like that..."

"...the Spurs will be heading to the NBA Championship series..."

Welcome to the 2005
NBA Championship
Finals

"It's Game 7 and it all ends tonight! Series play started off low and slow in San Antonio, then picked up some intensity in Detroit with the Pistons tying the series with 2 games each..."

"...then the Spurs handed a tough loss to the Pistons on their own court..."

"...only to lose the series lead when they returned to San Antonio..."

"...which is where we are this evening, and it all ends tonight!"

San Antonio Spurs: NBA Champs

2006

Malcolm Price is giving the lay of the land to his Mama Girl who's in from Lewisburg for the summer. "We're in Bastrop County now which is 80 miles northeast of San Antonio and 20 miles southeast of Austin. We'll stay on State Highway 21 for about 7 miles and be in Wyldwood in no time."

"Can't imagine I'll need all of this mileage and driving direction, but I sure do appreciate knowing."

Malcolm reaches across and takes his mother's hand, "I should have asked how your flight was."

"The first of anything is a wonder of things. I suspect I'll enjoy the trip home, and then be happy to stay put."

Malcolm laughs big, "Not a fan then."

"A fine description, son. You dealing with the playoff loss? Must have been bitter-tasting after last year's victory."

"Dealing some. It was tough, but playing in the All-Star game set things right."

"Good. When winning and losing are the only two options, you ought to set your mind for both."

Malcolm squeezes Mama Girl's hand.

She squeezes right back. "I've missed you son."

Reasons

Book 2

Malcolm and Sage

2007

Welcome to the 2007
NBA Championship Series
Western Conference – First Round

Malcolm Price, point guard for the San Antonio Spurs, should have his head in the game—it's a Championship playoff game against the Denver Nuggets, after all. The Spurs are up 3-1 in the series going into that night's duel, and with a win the team will put that round of play behind them. True to form, sports reporters herald the young phenom as one of the greatest to pound the parquet, then pick around the edges of his performance.

"...Malcolm Price didn't get the call until the 28th round in the 2003 NBA draft, but he sure is playing like the top seed..."
"...you're right Don. 77 has been pro for three years and this is his third year of Championship play..."
"...and so far, he's 1 for 2 in the winner takes all Finals. Price is holding his own during this year's post-season play, but it's clear 77 hasn't found IT yet."

The man who wears that number—the man who **is** that number—agrees with the critique. He hasn't found IT yet. He hopes tonight will change things—on and off the court.

The b-baller doesn't need to scan the arena for her, his eyes go to the seat she's been in for every series home game. He doesn't need to scan for him, either. Seated next to the girl is an angry pit bull of a man who simultaneously ignores her presence and pisses his territory around her. Malcolm pegs the extraordinarily beautiful young woman as a few years younger than his twenty-five years — pegs the pit bull as being in his thirties, and her 'John'.

The girl who's caught the player's eye is tall, almost as tall as the dog she's with, bringing her close to 6'. She has waist-length, stick-straight, black-as-coal hair, and bangs that brush across her brows. Her eyes are big and expressive; her face is oval and cut with high cheekbones; her smile is wide and toothy. She – Is – Beautiful, and she is aware she's caught the eye of the player wearing Spurs team jersey 77. The girl flashes him a smile, swings her hair over her shoulder and moves her bangs with her fingertips.

The player likes her smile and hair gesture, he especially likes the movement of the long black strands as they fall back into place.

The pit bull, on the other hand, likes none of it. He bangs his calloused fist onto her knee, takes hold of her thigh and squeezes tight. She winces and looks away from 77.

The pro pulls his attention from the girl and turns it to the reason he's standing center court—the game. He tries to put the noise out and focus in. A rather big call when he heard the talking heads say he's being hailed as a future Hall of Famer.

"...yeah those are big accolades for the kid from The Burg. Three years in and Malcolm Price is getting nods for a future slot in the Hall..."

"...that's because this player is serious about his game. He reads the action like few can, uses every bit of his brawn, can handle the hell out of the ball—and as far as on-court coaching is concerned, no one is better..."

"...most of the time..."

The tempo is slow and the final score low,
but the Spurs are heading to the
Conference Semifinals.

Before hitting the showers, Malcolm hangs back and watches from across the court as his assistant, Jason Carpenter, approaches the girl and her pit bull.

"77 would like you two to join him at the meet and greet," Jason addresses the scowling man and gently squeezes the girl's shoulder.

"Tell Price we're busy," the pit bull growls.

The girl searches and finds 77 from across the court. She brushes her bangs away from her eyes then turns them to the man still standing next to her, the one with his hand still on her shoulder.

Heckles from the crowd flanking the 'chosen two' quickly rise, "What are you nuts?" – "That's 77." – "What's this dude's fucking problem? The legendary point guard wants to meet you—you get off your fucking ass and meet him." – "The douchebag is probably afraid Price will take his girl." – "What a pussy."

The angry man bends to public pressure, turns and glares at 77. They hold one another's stare and nod their heads.

Game On!

The Malcolm Price waits just outside the meet and greet until the room is ready. Chants of, 77! .... 77! .... 77! .... start the same way after every win — slow and steady. The pace and intensity increases with every minute, until an excited roar thunders through the space. There is one thing, and one thing only, that can break the crescendo — the appearance of The Malcolm Price. When the b-baller thinks his fans have had their fill, he enters the room. The crowd erupts with final chants of 77! to which he answers, **"Is In The House!"** It's the same every time—and it never gets old. Not for the fans, not for The Malcolm Price.

The MAN easily finds the GIRL through the throng of revelers. He is slow getting to her. When he finally reaches the couple standing off to the side, he extends his right hand to the man, "Malcolm Price," while he palms his phone number to the girl. She discreetly tucks the piece of paper into the pocket of her Calvin knockoffs.

The pit bull reaches into his jacket pocket and hands the player a business card, "Micky Strong, PI. Let's talk about my services. A man of your fame and fortune must need issues worked out from time to time," the dick throws a tilt of his head toward the girl and a classless wink toward the star athlete.

The player ignores the drooling, panting dog and introduces himself to the girl. "Malcolm Price," he says with a wide smile.

"Sage Finley," she says with the dip of her head. "The game was a bit slow tonight, Mr. Price." She flashes a wide smile.

Malcolm laughs big.

The dick pulls her close.

The young player puts his gigantic hand onto the pit bull's shoulder and squeezes—a bit too tightly, "Good to meet you, both. Enjoy the party." With that, 77 walks into the crowd without so much as a look back.

Sage knowingly watches as the flock of females eye the 6'5" light-skinned black man as he moves through the room. His gait is graceful, yet edgy, like a panther who knows there is prey all around and that with minimal effort he can pounce and have what he wants. He seems not to want—at least not what is currently being offered. Sage mentally compares the casually dressed, relaxed Malcolm Price to the one who dominated the court pouring every ounce of sweat into the power of the game. She likes both sides of the young man, is particularly drawn to the twinkle of his light caramel-brown eyes and devilish grin as he charms and enjoys life around him.

The pit bull angrily interrupts her eyeful draw of 77, "Let's go." He grabs hold of her upper arm, squeezes way too tight, and pulls way too hard.

From Pembroke to Wyldwood.

The paying customer takes the working girl to one of the cheaper hotels on the preapproved list given out by the escort service, Garden of Eve. He bangs her as roughly as is allowed by the contract agreement he signed, tosses a twenty onto the bed, and makes for the door. "I need to see a bookie about some bucks; find your own ride back to whatever hell hole you call home."

As soon as Micky leaves, Sage goes to the bathroom, throws up, takes a shower, brushes her teeth, and pulls Malcolm Price's phone number from her pocket. She dials it without pause.

He answers on the fifth ring. "Price."

"Mr. Price, this is Sage Finley, I met you this evening."

"What can I do for you, Sage?"

"I need a ride home."

"Are you alone?"

"Yes."

"Where are you?"

"Pembroke Hotel on…"

"I know the place," Malcolm interrupts. "Room number?"

"212."

"Stay inside. I'll be there in twenty minutes. Don't let him back in." Malcolm knocks on the hotel room door fifteen minutes later. "It's 77."

Sage opens the door.

The MAN is pushed back by her beauty, angered by other things.

Sage is dressed in the same outfit as earlier in the evening, but she's accessorized with a few new things—a red grab mark on her bicep and a handprint across her face.

"Get your things," he says through clenched teeth.

She wags her purse toward him, "This is it."

The unsmiling man takes her hand and leads her out of the fleabag hotel and to his Mercedes parked around the corner. He opens her door then heads to his. As he climbs in, he sees the pit bull heading back inside the hotel.

The young woman sees him too. She pushes low into her seat and shivers.

"Where to, Sage?" He starts the Mercedes and pulls out of the parking lot.

"Tucks," is all she says. It's all she needs to say.

Malcolm eyes her. "You live in the projects? Those projects? Pretty rough place. You live there alone?"

"I do now that Momma died." Sage turns to look out the side window...

"Sage," the young medical student said softly.

Sage roused from her tortured sleep, "Momma?" her voice caught with fear.

"She wants you to be with her now."

"It's time?" tears filled Sage's eyes. Sympathy filled those of the young professional who came to escort a child to her momma's deathbed.

Malcolm notices the sudden tears that wet Sage's eyes as she turns away. He picks up his cell and presses a number, "Hey, Sammi, I need a place near the ranch."

"For tonight?" the woman asks.

"Indefinitely," he replies and hangs up.

"You missed the turnoff to Tucks, Mr. Price."

"We're going to dinner, first."

Tucks

Micky Strong parks his Lincoln at the curb in front of Sage's squalor place. The paying customer of the escort service isn't supposed to know where his girl-for-hire lives, but the PI followed Sage home after their first night together and a couple of times since then. Micky **hates** bringing his ride into the shithole projects, but he paid for a night with the whore and he is gonna get his money's worth. His anger is full-on now. He's pissed at the ribbing he took from the fans at the Center, pissed that 77 dismissed him after a brief introduction, and beyond pissed that his whore left Pembroke. "You owe me a night of fucking bitch and I'm gonna get every penny's worth, but it's not gonna be here."

Micky bangs on the door of shithole #11, bangs again, and again. A dog from up the street responds unfavorably to the disturbance, causing a few lights to flick on inside a few of the other numbered shitholes. Micky continues taking his frustration out on the door until someone yells, "Bang one more time muthafucka and I'll blow your fuckin head off." The pissed man bangs one last time and shouts, "Fuck you!" as he heads to his car and peels out of Tucks—as much as a big ass Lincoln can peel out, that is.

I-35N
Malcolm Price pulls to a stop and opens his door to get out. Sage opens her door to get out.

"Shut the door, Sage."

She does as she is told.

The tall, powerful man rounds the Benz and opens the passenger door. He offers the young woman his gigantic hand; she slips hers in and lets him help her out. He places his hand to the small of her back and leads her inside a roadside burger joint—somewhere between San Antonio and Austin. The patrons clap and shout as the couple moves past.

"Good game 77," a group of cowboys call out. "Made me a damn good penny on you tonight."

Malcom smiles, "Made a damn good penny for myself tonight."

"You're bringing it home this year, Malcolm," an older than dirt, near toothless man smiles. "The Title, man, it's yours for the taking."

"We'll see, Willie," Malcolm smiles wide. "What're you having tonight?"

"Pie and tea. Best pie in the world."

"Have a burger first. Best burger in the world." Malcolm eyes the cook who nods.

"Take a seat, Sugar, I'll be over for your order in a few," a squat waitress with tree-stump legs and thick waist calls out. It's straight up obvious that this waitress thinks of the diner as her home and the customers as her family.

"I'll take my usual Marge," the regular smiles wide. "What would you like, Sage?"

"Toast and tea, please."

"You heard the lady, Marge?"

"Heard her fine, 77."

He grabs a booth in the back.

"You come here a lot," Sage says, barely above a whisper.

"It's between where I work and where I live."

The wary young woman takes a look around, "Mr. Price, I need to get back to San Antonio and check in with the service."

He hands her his cell phone. "Call them. Tell them you quit."

Sage drops the fork she's been nervously twirling. "I can't quit," she says on an exhaled laugh.

Malcolm slides his phone toward her. "Call."

She reaches for his cell, halts when she sees the tremble in her hand. She looks at her non-paying escort for reassurance.

He nods. "Call."

The working girl picks up the phone, puts it back on the table when Marge brings their food. They are just finishing their meals when Malcolm receives a call. "Sammi, what have you got?" He listens. "Sounds good. Rent it, put everything in your name, I don't want her or me traceable, and text me the address. Bring the keys to the Center at 10 AM, and clear your schedule for a few days. Thanks, Sammi."

He turns his attention to Sage. "You have a new place to live. Do you need anything from Tucks?"

"Mr. Price, could you please explain what's going on?"

"You are out of the business and it's Malcolm." He smiles w.i.d.e. hoping to take the edge off.

"Am I going to be your personal escort?" she asks tentatively.

"Maybe later. Right now, you need to be away from the dick."

Sage reflexively rubs her bicep and nods. "I need my Momma's ashes from Tucks."

"I'll have someone take you when I'm at the Center tomorrow." He taps his phone. "Make the call."

She does as she is told.

They arrive late to Malcolm's guarded ranch in Wyldwood, Texas, a town of less than 1,000 in Bastrop County. They walk in silence through a massive wood-everywhere structure and climb a very wide center staircase to a balcony-wrap that heads off in two directions. Malcolm shows Sage to her room, kisses her cheek, and leaves.

Soft rugs and busted linoleum.

Morning comes early for the rescued girl. She pulls her pillow from beneath her head and presses it tightly behind her back. From upon the massive four-poster, canopied wonderland of fluffy bed linens in pale yellows, happy pinks, and muted greens, Sage takes in the splendor of the room. It is big and fancy and holds furniture that is big and fancy. She moves slowly and softly off the bed – so as not to disturb the wonderful dream she surely must be having. Her feet land gently on a patterned floral rug, the kind of which she's never seen or felt. She squishes her toes into the springy softness, then pads quietly along stopping at massive side by side windows. She opens one and is greeted by a gentle breeze that lifts fancy lacy curtains that flutter across her face as she looks out over beautifully manicured land for as far as the eye can see. The young woman twists herself into the white lace then unfurls and scampers to the other side of the room. She bends low and inspects the pretty things on display. Braided fringe on a shaded lamp skips through her outstretched fingers. Fragrant tiny buds in tiny painted vases, and fragrant potpourri chips in a cut-crystal footed bowl tickle her senses. "This room doesn't feel like a guest room, it feels as though it's laid out for someone special; someone who hasn't come yet or someone who's come and gone."

The wondering wanderer pinches herself so often during her tour that a welt forms on her thigh; she notices a nearby bruise from where Micky squeezed her when he caught her looking at 77 from across the arena. She rubs the sore spots then moves her hand from her leg to her bicep. The squeeze Micky gave her is black and blue now. Her hand trembles as she traces his thumbprint, then freezes in place at the sound of a knock on her door.

"Sage."

"Yes?" she ekes out.

"We leave in an hour. There's breakfast downstairs; eat something."

The nauseated young woman runs to the bathroom at the thought of food. She dry heaves then puts her head onto the cold porcelain. She silently laments, "He'll make me leave when I tell him."

Tucks

At 7 AM, before the project fully wakes for the day, Micky Strong picks the lock on shithole #11. He enters directly into a ratty kitchen with torn linoleum and appliances that might work. He walks past a half-wall into a ratty living room that has a ratty recliner and a cot with ratty linen and nothing else. His tour of the place where Sage lived and her mother inched toward death leads him to a bedroom the size of a closet, with nothing in it but a mattress, a couple bureau drawers, and stacks and stacks of beat up old books. His final stop is at a clean but worn-torn bathroom. The PI checks the bottles that line a single shelf in a doorless medicine cabinet, finds nothing but over the counter stuff. He is about to leave when a box resting on a tiny painted-shut window ledge catches his eye. He grabs it and reads the label, "Early Announcement." He angrily bangs his fist against the wall, knocking some plaster free, "A fucking pregnancy test." The pissed-off man rummages through a waste basket and pulls an obviously pissed-upon stick that sports a blue equal sign. He reads the box for confirmation. "Someone's having a baby and it sure ain't the whore's dead mother." Micky puts the used test into the box, takes it with and leaves the ratty shithole.

By noon, Micky has placed his fourth call to Garden of Eve asking for a date with Sage. For the fourth time, Eve Lappier tells him Sage quit the business.

Micky flips his shit.

I-35S
"Tell me about yourself."

"Nothing interesting about my life, Malcolm. Momma got pregnant at sixteen, Baby Daddy left her before she was showing, she got kicked out of her house and had to scrounge for places to crash until she had me. When she got assistance from the State, she moved us into Tucks where we lived happily ever after." She glances at the fine black man driving the Mercedes.

He glances back, "I said tell me about you, Sage."

"Oh, well, in that case my story is so much better. I got the tar beat out of me by girls at school because I was a straight-A student. When I got boobs, I went from girls beating me to boys helping themselves to me. My grades suffered, my attitude hit the shits, and I wanted away from it all. I was ready to bail on life at Tucks when Momma got sick and had to leave her job at the corner mart." The young woman pulls a shaky breath before continuing. "I quit school, took Momma's job to put food on the table, and when the money didn't cover her medical needs, I took a job at the escort service, even though she begged me not to. Momma died six weeks ago. Like I said, happily ever after," she chokes and turns away…

"Sage? Is that you?"

"Momma? What are you doing up? You should be resting."

"It's late Sage."

The young woman knew where the conversation was headed. "Not too late, Momma."

"The Mart closed hours ago. Where? Where have you been? Please tell me you're not…"

"Momma," Sage sat next to her mother's cot, "I'm not turning tricks."

The dying woman closed her eyes. The effort nearly too much for her weary self. She pushed out a few words, important words, desperate words. "Sage, the medicine. It's not helping. Don't buy anymore. Please stop doing what you're doing. Please."

"But Momma."

"Please, Sage."

Malcolm reaches across the car and places his hand on the weeping girl's knee, "You're with me now."

She places her hand on top of his and pushes her words through a bit of ugly crying. "I know you are trying to make a difference in my life, though I don't know why." She wraps her fingers around his and gives a small squeeze. The corners of her lips turn upward as a final tear slides down her cheek, "I can't get out of my life, Malcolm. It's already heading for disaster. I couldn't afford Momma's medicine **and** my birth control; I chose Momma's medicine. I'm pregnant with Micky's kid." Sage lets go of Malcolm's hand.

He pulls it back and gives it a tender squeeze, "What do you want to do, Sage?"

"I don't want it, but if I don't have it and Micky finds out, He. Will. Kill. Me."
"Then he doesn't find out."

Am I dreaming?

Sammi Wilcox is leaning against her 2006 silver hybrid Lexus when Malcom arrives at the AT&T Center. She has with her a set of keys to an adorable garden cottage in Wyldwood not too far from Malcolm's ranch, and is wearing a wide smile on her face. As owner of Earth Homes Realty, Sammi caters to a niche clientele – the environmentally conscious rancher who wants to work the land **and** protect it. She loves her job and her life, but the thing Sammi takes greatest pride in, is her friendship with 77. She'd do just about anything for the man, like clear her schedule and spend the day with his new friend.

Malcolm introduces the women then hands Sammi a credit card, "Get Sage whatever she wants for her place and whatever she needs for herself. Have Jason get her a cell phone, computer, printer and set them up. There's something Sage wants from Tucks, have Jason go, not you two. After you shop, take her to the new place and get her settled in. Thanks, Sammi."

Malcolm kisses Sage on the cheek. "I'll stop by, later." He opens the passenger door, waits for her to settle in, then closes it behind her.

The dazed young woman waits until The Malcolm Price disappears inside the Center, then asks the woman she's known for a handful of seconds, "Am I dreaming?"

Sammi offers a wide smile and a one word answer, "Nope."

Garden Oasis

The one-bedroom garden cottage, just off the main thoroughfare in Wyldwood, was once a guest house at the Pendleton Place. Congressman Walt Pendleton and his wife, Mavis, moved into Oasis after a fire burned the main house to the ground. When the owners retired to sunny Florida from sunny Texas they listed the property for sale with Earth Homes— then had a change of heart about selling. The former statesman asked Sammi to contract caretakers for the place and gave her authority to lease it, "Should the right renter come along."

Sammi contacted the folks right after Malcom's call from the diner the night before. "Mavis, it's Sammi. The right tenant has come along for Garden Oasis. The person responsible for the lease would prefer anonymity."

The realtor never said, and the owners never asked, but any gambler worth his or her weight in poker chips would have been all-in that the renter is Malcolm Price. Like everyone else in Wyldwood and in the County of Bastrop, Walt and Mavis Pendleton love 77, they protect his privacy, and they take great pride that he chose their little corner of Texas for his home — they just don't tell anyone. That's why the retired folks agreed to put the rental agreement in Sammi's name making her the responsible party of Garden Oasis.

Sammi turns off the thoroughfare onto a narrow pebble path, travels a bit, then comes to a stop in front of a 1,000 square foot storybook cottage surrounded by white picket fences all ablaze with bright yellow trumpet-shaped flowers spreading full across thick, lush vines.

"Oh, Sammi. Look at those flowers. They're beautiful, and plentiful. What are they?"

"Carolina Jessamine."

"Carolina Jessamine," she whispers, "such a pretty name."

Sammi nudges Sage's shoulder and points to the pale yellow abode, trimmed in white and dark green set behind the floral-covered picket fence. "That's your new home."

"It's idyllic," Sage exhales on a sigh.

"Come on. I'll show you around."

The front door opens into the living room that holds an overstuffed floral upholstered couch, a white rocking chair with a matching floral cushion, and a small entertainment center with television and stereo system. The kitchen is separated from the living room by a half-wall with tall stools on the living room side and a café table and chairs on the kitchen side. The appliances are white, the walls are cream, and the terrace off the kitchen is to die for. Clay pots of every size and shape fill the space and are filled with flowers of every color and fragrance imaginable.

"The terrace is going to be my favorite spot," Sage enthuses to Sammi.

"I can see why, it's really beautiful and tranquil. You'll have to tend the pots, Sage."

"Oh, I will. I never have, but I'll learn." Sage walks the length of the space to a French door that leads out to a fieldstone walking path surrounded by tall flower hedges and adorned with stone sitting benches, birdbaths, and garden ornaments. "I'll tend these, too, Sammi."

"There's an outdoor crew, Sage, but if you're serious, ask Luke for gardening tips. He works here and at Malcolm's ranch."

"He's the gardener?"

"Horticulturist. He does everything, planting, growing, tending, landscape design, the whole lot of it."

"A horticulturist," Sage whispers.

The women backtrack through the terrace and continue the tour. The bedroom off the living room easily takes up most of the cottage's square footage. "Oh, Sammi, this is a place for quiet reflection. I think Malcolm will love this room. I know I don't know him, but I can see him here."

The bedroom differs greatly from the living room. There is nothing fussy about the space. The walls are a deep beige, the furniture is simple Shaker, and the fixtures and lamps are hand-rubbed bronze. There is a sitting area for two near a corner fireplace, and a nearby built-in bookcase filled with hardcovers. The king-sized bed is set on a one-step-up platform, and the en suite bathroom, done in earth tones and bronze is positively luxurious. A French door, very similar to the one off the terrace, leads to a small patio where a black wrought iron table and chair set, and an awning-covered glider for two waits for enjoyment.

Sage inches her way through the room, ending her stroll at the fireplace, "Am I to tend to the fire, too? I haven't a clue how and would probably set all of this wonder in flames."

Sammi laughs, "It's an electric fireplace. The owners learned from experience."

Sage raises a brow in question.

"The Pendleton Place, the estate that used to be set on the front part of the property burned to the ground years ago. Walt and Mavis Pendleton moved into Garden Oasis before retiring to Florida. They wanted fireside relaxation without the worry."

"The fireplace is electrical?"

Sammi walks to the unit, flicks a switch and voilà a warm amber glow appears from behind a beveled glass front as heat pushes forth.

Sage plops onto one of the chairs, "I'm in a dream. I must be in a dream."

Sammi gives Sage's foot a tap, "Come on, let's set the place before Malcolm gets here."

A squeal of excitement erupts as the girl buzzes from room to room putting this here and that there. Most of her time is spent in the bedroom laying out moss green sheets, a cream comforter, and throw pillows of black, green, and cream stripped satin. Her final touch is a black picture frame, three tiny painted bud vases, and a cut-crystal footed bowl for the end table, "Oh, Sammi, I forgot to buy the smell-good chips to put into the bowl."

"I have some at the bunkhouse. I'll bring them next time I come."

"Perfect." The last thing Sage takes from her shopping bag is the first thing she chose, a man's terrycloth robe. She runs her hands over the nappy fiber before hanging it in her closet. A smile, the one Malcolm Price first noticed from across a basketball court in an arena with twenty thousand fans, takes hold of Sage's face, "Oh, Sammi. This is the most exciting thing I have ever done. I can't wait for Malcolm to see this splendor."

At the sound of a knock later that day, Sage swings the door wide — Malcolm is waiting on the other side and he **is not** happy.

"Don't answer the door without checking," he warns.

"I knew it was you."

"No, you didn't."

Sage lets him pass through, shuts the door behind him, and leans back against it. She watches as the M.A.N tours the space.

"It came furnished?"

She nods.

"If you want something different, tell Sammi. The bedroom looks nice. Jason got your things from Tucks."

"I don't know. I haven't seen Jason today."

"It wasn't a question, Girl." Malcolm hands off a small duffle bag, "Jason got your momma."

Sage's hand trembles as she unzips the bag. She peeks inside not quite sure what she'll find; silently processes upon the sight, then lifts a beautiful shiny gold urn from within. "This is Momma? Oh, Malcolm. What a refined display. So much more fitting than that wooden box." While Sage walks the place contemplating the perfect resting place for Momma, Malcolm continues his look around.

"The picture on the nightstand. Is that yours?" he asks when he rejoins her.

Sage laughs, "Yes. The picture inside is of Jessica and Alex." She lowers her voice a bit,

"Those are the names I've given them." She smiles wide and continues. "I've decided they live in Washington, the state of not the District of. Jessica is an artist and does the most beautiful landscapes of the northwest, and Alex is a pilot. Jessica misses him when he flies, but she really appreciates the alone time," Sage smiles and winks. "For her painting, of course."

The man shakes his head—but as he turns to continue his inspection, she sees his smile. It's difficult to miss Malcolm's smile. Then, as quickly as it comes, it goes.

"Sage, the terrace doors need to be secured. Tell Sammi to have Jason do it and to put in a security system." He walks the space again. "The place suits you."

"Perfectly," she replies. "Thank you, Malcolm..." she pauses.

He notices the pause, "What?"

"There's a bookcase – in the bedroom – it's full of books. Do you think Mr. and Mrs. Pendleton would mind if I read one or two?"

"Read as many as you'd like, Sage. You like to read."

"Yes."

"It wasn't a question, Girl. Jason saw your stack of books at Tucks. He brought them for you."

"Really?"

He nods. "Have you eaten?"

She shakes her head. "I can't even think about food right now."

He moves to the kitchen and rummages through the cupboards. "You'll have soup, come sit while I get it for you."

She does as she is told.

Though unsure of the parameters of their relationship, Sage asks what's on her mind. "The room I stayed in last night; it seems as though it is decorated for someone special, it is very beautiful."

"It's Mama Girl's room. My mother's room. She doesn't come to Texas very often, so it doesn't get used much. Mama Girl says family should stay in the background when greatness is being pursued."

"Thank you for letting me use it last night."

"You're like Mama Girl was at your age, alone and trying hard to make it," he says as he puts the soup in front of her. He reaches into his pocket and hands her a card. "If you want an abortion, that doctor can handle it. Your decision, but I want you checked out to make sure you're healthy."

"You mean clean?" Sage corrects.

"That, too." Malcolm places a kiss on Sage's head and walks away. "I'll be back tomorrow. Don't answer that door to anyone but me, Sammi or Jason."

Don't. Fuck. With. Me.

Eve Lappier, owner and operator of the Garden of Eve escort service lets out an exasperated groan when Micky Strong slams out of his big-ass Lincoln and follows her to the front door of her place. "Micky. I still haven't heard from Sage and you're really starting to piss me off."

"Don't give a fuck, Eve. Someone must have heard something from the whore."

"Gee, I wonder why she up and left your ass."

"Don't. Fuck. With. Me. If she hasn't called in yet, she will. And when she does, you're gonna call me."

"She already quit. What makes you think she'll call in?"

"Did you pay her for that night?"

"No."

"Then she'll be by for her money."

Eve shrugs her shoulder.

"The only reason she wouldn't come by is if she went off with 77."

She shrugs again.

"Is that what you think?"

"I don't think anything, Micky. You're the one who said that's where she went. But if she did, she ain't coming back for the shit money she makes around here."

Micky closes the space between them, towers over the petite brunette as she pushes back tight against the wall. He leans low and threatens, "You tell that bitch **I know**, and that she'd better get her fucking ass back here." Micky stands tall and steps back at the warning whoop from a police car that's pulled in behind him.

Eve turns her back to Micky, puts the key in the lock, steps past the enraged man, and locks the door from the inside.

Micky swings his Lincoln out onto Stark Street and heads to Pembroke. He waits for the check-in clerk to arrive for her shift then makes his move. "I've been by a few times, Shirl."

"Yeah? What do you want?"

"Who'd Sage leave with last night?"

"Wasn't you, that's for **damn** sure."

"Don't. Fuck. With. Me."

"She left with 77. Couldn't hardly believe it was him, but there ain't no mistaking **that** man for any other."

"Fuck you, Shirl."

"Backatcha, Micky."

The increasingly pissed PI makes a swing through Tucks, takes several passes by the arena, and a few past the Haskin building looking for Price's Mercedes. He craps out at each location.

Alamo Heights
Malcolm headed back to the Center after seeing Sage. He's back in his car and cruising around San Antonio, making a bit of a show. He's sure the big-ass Lincoln he's been intersecting with – here and there – belongs to Micky Strong. "Good. If you're following me in San Antonio, then you don't know about Wyldwood—yet." A conversation he had earlier with Jason starts looping…

"She's safe in Wyldwood for now, Malcolm, but…"

"It won't work long-term."

"No one's had cause to care where you live. Mostly because people think they know – 77 lives at Alamo. But you're on the radar of Micky Strong, now, and he's not likely to stop looking for Sage, and…"

"…he knows she's with me."

Malcolm hits scan on his radio – stops its search at the soulful sound of Percy Sledge's *When a Man Loves a Woman*. Seconds in, he knows it's a cover—a **good** cover. He listens through, "Damn, Michael Bolton. Not bad for a white boy," he laughs. When he's had his fill of cruising and crooning, he pulls into the underground garage at his condo building. A half-hour later, he steps out onto his balcony for a look around. He easily finds the Lincoln in a parking lot across the street. Malcolm takes a long pull from his beer, and sits his ass for a spell, "Better to have him here than there."

No fairytale endings.

Sage waits until 10 AM before calling Sammi about the terrace doors and the security system. By early afternoon, a team of workers are drilling this and hammering that and by 5 PM they're gone. Sage is tidying the place when she hears Malcolm's car purr up the pebble driveway. She races to the door and pulls it open. Remembering his directive, she slams the door shut in his face and waits.

"Open the door, Sage," he says on a laugh.

"Who is it?" she teases.

Malcolm turns the knob and opens the door for himself. He smiles at the beautiful girl standing in front of him, then scowls, "Keep the door locked."

She rolls her eyes. "I grew up in the projects, Malcolm."

"Keep the door locked, Girl." He walks past her and calls over his shoulder, "Have you eaten today?"

"Yes," she lies.

"Are you lying to me, Girl?"

"Yes. I'm sorry, Malcolm, I just can't."

"Sit. I brought you square salty crackers and peaches. Mama Girl said you'll keep them down."

"You told your mother about me?"

"Tell her everything." He points to a chair, "Sit." Malcolm leans against a counter, crosses one ankle over the other, and watches Sage nibble the crackers and peaches.

"Tell your mother thank you for me," she flashes a toothy grin. "They are settling my stomach some, and I think they're staying put."

"How old are you?"

"Nineteen."

"How far along are you?"

"I don't really know how they calculate it, but I'm six weeks late on my period. I'm calling Monday for an appointment."

Malcolm nods. "Sammi will take you and stay with you. I won't be around much. The Semis start Sunday. You need anything, call Sammi or Jason. Keep the door locked and use the security system. Come here. I want to taste you."

Sage walks the few steps to him, places a foot on either side of his crossed feet, and presses against him. His excitement is long and hard along her belly. He skips his fingertips across her bangs, then runs his hand the length of her long hair before cupping the back of her head. He kisses her long and deep, groaning long and deep. "I want to do things with you, Sage, but you're in no condition, and there are things about this arrangement you need to understand. You are not my whore. You have a say in what we do if we do. When you want out, you're out. There isn't a fairytale ending in this fairytale cottage. If you fall in love, you will end up being hurt. Think about it when I'm gone."

He pushes himself to a full stand causing Sage to pull away. Again, he fingers her bangs and runs his hand the full length of her silky strands before leaving a kiss on her cheek. He walks to the door calling over his shoulder, "Eat while I'm gone. Get over here. Lock the door, and put on security."

She does as she is told.

Wyldwood Ranch
Sammi Wilcox is woken by a call from Sage Finley at 2:22 AM. The sleepy woman hears noises in the background, but no words coming over the line. "Sage, what's wrong?" Sammi bolts from the bed she shares with Jason Carpenter, Malcolm's assistant, drags her clothes off the floor and onto her body. "I'm on my way, Jason is coming with."

Sammi Wilcox and Jason Carpenter are opposites in every way imaginable, but they couldn't be more suited to one another. She is an earth-crunching, hybrid-driving, plant-eating vegan. He is an earth-working, Mustang-riding, beef-eating cowboy. They live together in a converted workhand bunkhouse at the forefront of Wyldwood Ranch and have been together since the day Malcolm signed the Purchase and Sale agreement for the McCaid spread…

"Want to meet your herd, Mr. Price?"

"Malcolm," he nodded.

The men headed to a Jeep – Sammi headed to her car, then answered, "Hell, yeah," when asked if she wanted to ride along.

Jason drove the trio away from the main house and its manicured lawns toward open fields that edged along a 480-foot wide section of Cantor River. The man who'd worked the land at Wyldwood for more than a decade gave the lay of the land to the new owner. "Your spread looks like a blunt-edged triangle. The front end of the property is the narrowest part, and from where you turn off the thoroughfare to where we are now, it's approximately seventy-five acres…"

"Seventy-seven acres," 77 interrupted.

"Well, I'll be damned," Jason gave his head a good shake and prattled on. "The back three-hundred+ acres can be accessed from this side by using a split-log bridge, or at the west end trail that cuts through some shallow waters, or by getting yourself mighty wet with a swim. The bridge is used by me and the residents of the main house. Your ranch hands live and work that side of the river and don't usually head this way. The only exception to all that is Luke Haynes. You'll see him all over the ranch. He handles everything from seeding to harvesting the few crop fields we run, but he's mostly responsible for maintaining the marginal land."

"The Longhorn grazing land," **Malcolm offered.**

Jason smiled wide. "You've got twenty-five each of purebred Texas Longhorns and American Angus crossbreds. We graze a dozen head for Don Lyle, and work your spread right for you, Malcolm."

As the ranch hand talked to the new owner, he checked the rearview for an eyeful of the woman riding along. He liked what he saw— a woman who wore the hell out of her Wranglers, had long, crinkled, blonde hair, golden-brown eyes, and a smile that said she was enjoying his attention. After taking the new owner for a ride around the property, Jason took Sammi for a ride in his bed. She has been there ever since.

Jason bangs on the cottage door then keys the lock. He goes to the security panel, sees that it's off, pulls a gun from the waistband of his jeans and quickly scans the place for intruders. Sammi runs past him and finds Sage on the bathroom floor curled into a fetal position, panting through uterine contractions—her body's way of handling the problem pregnancy. Jason lifts Sage from the floor as Sammi goes in search of something to wrap around the miscarrying woman's sweat-and-blood-stained nightgown. She grabs a black terry-cloth robe from the closet and tucks it tight around the trembling young woman.

"Sage, we're taking you to Bastrop Medical." Sammi hops into the backseat, puts Sage's head onto her lap, and gently strokes it while a life seeps from the young woman's womb.

The medical team helps Sage with her miscarriage care, gives her a thorough examination, runs a series of tests, pushes IV fluids, and keeps her for observation until early evening. When Jason escorts Sammi and Sage into Garden Oasis, all telltale signs of what happened are gone. The linen on the bed has been replaced, the bathroom has been scoured, vases of flowers are placed throughout the cottage, and there is a big pot of chicken stew on the stove. The very grateful woman thanks him for all the effort, then walks to her room and closes the door. Within an hour, Sammi knocks and enters the darkened room. She turns on a bedside lamp and finds Sage in the same fetal position as the night before. She rushes to the far side of the bed.

"Are you all right, do you need to go back to Bastrop Medical?"

Sage unfurls herself, leaves her hand pressed tight to her abdomen. "No, just some cramping, they said to expect it. I was just thinking, is all."

"Well, you're going to have to do that thinking at the ranch. Malcolm doesn't want you left alone and this place doesn't have room for Jason and me, so we need to get moving. Do you need me to do anything for you?"

Sage pulls herself to her feet, bends a bit, then shakes her head no.

The exhausted young woman settles at the ranch pretty quick and is in a deep sleep in Mama Girl's room when Malcolm returns to the ranch. She stirs when his fingers brush away bangs from her forehead. She opens her eyes, shakes her head, and closes them again.

"Come here, Girl."

Sage leans into him. He wraps her tight and lets her cry.

"Mama Girl said you'll feel the loss," he whispers.

"Even though I didn't want it?" she asks through sobs.

"Even though." Malcolm holds Sage until she falls back to sleep and until the next morning's light.

Welcome to the 2007
NBA Championship Series
Western Conference – Semifinals

Malcolm enters the Center ready for Game One of the Semis against the Phoenix Suns. He knows Micky Strong is in the stands; he can feel the intensity of the pit bull's stares. The b-baller ignores the dick until his number is announced:

"... and wearing San Antonio Spurs team jersey 77, Theeeee Malcom Price!"

The point guard takes center court, tosses a wave to the standing crowd, then narrows his eyes on Micky. He gives an extra wide smile and swishes an imaginary ball in his direction.
The. Crowd. Goes. Wild.
Micky gets up and storms from the arena.

Paula's on the Chase
The sports bar in downtown San Antonio is packed full of rowdy revelers, all stomping and chanting, "77! 77! 77!" The thunderous noise shakes the place from wall to wall and floor to ceiling. Micky seethes into his booze, occasionally glancing at one of three widescreen TVs, all tuned in to the game, all filled with images of Malcolm Price. The pissed

PI tosses back the whiskey part of his third Boilermaker, takes a quick breather, then finishes with the beer chaser.

"Fucking Price took my whore," he slurs at the barkeep who takes his empties and points to the door.

"Time to leave, Micky."

The pissed as a fart patron tosses a wad of cash onto the bar, mumbles something about getting his bitch back under control, and storms out of Paula's, just as the final buzzer claims victory for the Spurs.

Garden Oasis

Sage was on her feet for most of the game, well, except for the times when cramping took hold and she needed to sit. But other than that, she was like every other Spurs fan—on her feet and chanting, "77! 77! 77!" The tempo was up, the crowd was wild, and Malcolm was doing IT. He calls her cell before hitting the showers. "Micky's pissed. Lock up."

"I already did, Malcolm," Sage whispers to dead air.

San Antonio

Micky pulls his hangdog ass from bed Monday afternoon, runs his hand over his pit bull face, throws himself into the rumpled clothes he'd strewn across the floor the night before, grabs his keys, and heads to his Lincoln. He calls his good-for-almost-nothing computer whiz nephew, Stoner. "Meet me at the office and bring your computer."

Stoner, who hadn't had a facial expression in years, looks positively gobsmacked when Micky gives him a very specific job. "Do whatever the fuck you do with that computer of yours, and get shit on Malcolm Price. I don't fucking care if you end up in hacker's prison, get me every fucking thing there is on that muthafucka!"

"Shit. Hacker's prison. Not gonna happen. FICA can't touch me," the nephew boasts.

"What's FICA?"

"The FBI division that handles cyber shit. They can't put my ass in hacker's prison if they can't get shit on me." He scoffs at his uncle, "You don't know shit about hacking do you?"

"I know I'm gonna fuck you up if you say another word." Micky swipes his arm across his desk sending all his stuff flying. "Sit the fuck down, get the fuck to work. And if FICA busts your ass, you're on your own. I'll be in the Lincoln, call me with the shit." The PI storms out and drives to Tucks for another look around.

Wyldwood
Sage eases back into Sammi's waiting Lexus after coming from her follow-up doctor's appointment. She received a clean bill of health, both from the post-miscarriage end of things,

and the 'you don't have any sexual scourges' end of things. After a girls' lunch out, Sage heads to the terrace for an afternoon with her precious array of floral friends. After a formal introduction on their first day together, Sage has taken to calling each by name, and telling them stories — much like the stories she told her momma before things got bad.

"You know, Miss Rose, flowers weren't a thing where I grew up." A little water here, a little turn of a pot there, "It wasn't until I started tending to you beauties, Miss Poppy, that I learned flowers came in a variety of shapes, colors, and fragrances. I mean, *I knew*. I'd seen pictures, of course. And there was that one day, Miss Lily, when I stopped in a flower shop, just by chance when the crosstown bus broke down. I saw wonderous flowers that day, Miss Iris." A little touch here, a little sniff there, "And one Valentine's Day, Mrs. Jackson, she was my Grade 7 math teacher, a truly horrible woman, but apparently not too horrible to get flowers delivered to school. When I saw them on her desk, Miss Daisy, I just had to have one so I snuck in and pulled one from the vase." A little pinch of a deadhead here, a little snip of a bloom there, "If I'd been caught, Miss Marigold, I surely would've been riding the bench outside the principal's office until Momma got there for a shared lecture." Sage wipes a tear from her cheek leaving a smudge of dirt behind, gathers herself and her thoughts and continues her prattle. "So, where was I, oh, right, so I've *seen* flowers before, Miss Violet, but I've never really *seen* flowers before."

The captivated young woman decides she wants to know everything there is to know about gardening. That evening, she sits crossed-legged on her overstuffed floral upholstered couch and does search after internet search on everything related to horticulture. "Hmmmm. It's a serious thing." She opens a website and reads, "Horticulture; the growing of flowers, fruits and vegetables for foods and ornamentals…plant conservation, landscape restoration and design, soil management…" Sometime after midnight, the budding horticulturist falls into a wonderful dream about meadows, tree sprites, and garden gnomes.

Arizona

Malcolm calls Sage from Phoenix before the game starts, "Doing good, Girl?"

"Doing good. I'll be watching," her voice fills with excitement.

"You should. I got IT back," 77 announces. "I'll be at your place tomorrow night at eight. Wait for my knock."

Malcolm Price has IT back, and then some.
The Spurs win by twenty points.

Garden Oasis

Sage is at the door waiting for Malcolm's knock—it comes at 8 PM. "I wonder who ever could be at my door, a gentleman caller, perhaps?" Sage teases.

"Open up, Girl," Malcolm laughs from the other side.

The very excited young woman swings the door wide and throws herself into Malcolm's arms. "Only you could shade the Sun, 77. Great game." She kisses him deep and long and rubs her hips suggestively against his length.

Malcolm's response is immediate, "Don't you need time to recover?"

Sage starts working Malcolm's jeans, "Nothing wrong with my mouth, Malcolm."

He stops her downward trajectory, "I'm big."

Sage flashes him a wide toothy grin, "I can handle you, big boy."

Sage handles the hell out of Malcolm right there in front of the unlocked door.

He knows.

Micky Strong pushes hard against the eager fans at the Center's entrance. When he makes it inside, he scans the crowd – practically growls when he finds the dude who offered the meet and greet invitation from Price. He waits until Jason walks past then steps in behind him. "Tell Price I'm coming for my bitch and my baby," Micky has his say, then pushes past.

Jason follows the PI inside the arena, grabs himself some leaning space along a wall, and places a call when there's five minutes left on the game clock. "I need eyes on a private dick who goes by the name Micky Strong. He's in section 109, row 1, seat 11. Make sure he leaves the Center, then follow him." At the sound of the buzzer Jason goes to the meet and greet. Malcolm is riding high from the decided win over the Suns—until he sees the expression on his friend's face. He motions for Jason to meet him outside the room.

"Talk to me."

"Micky Strong gave me a message for you, 'he's coming for his bitch and his baby'. He knows."

Malcolm reaches into his pocket, hands Jason the keys to the Mercedes, and takes a set of keys for Jason's Ford F-150. "Take Micky on a little trip through Texas. I'll be at the cottage with Sage."

Oasis

Sage kills the lights and crouches low at the front door when she hears a vehicle on the pebble driveway—a vehicle that does not have the purr of Malcom's Mercedes. She eyes the security panel over her shoulder just to make sure she remembered to activate it. She had. She turns her head in the direction of footfalls heading her way, holds her breath when they land on the tiny front porch. Relief floods at the sound of Malcom's knocked announcement.

"Sage, it's 77."

The terrified woman pulls herself up, unbolts the door, bangs the security panel, and steps back from Malcolm's approaching form.

"Micky knows about the pregnancy," he says as he kicks the door closed behind him.

Sage begins to shake, then paces the room. "He won't believe I miscarried, he's gonna think I got rid of it. He's gonna kill me, Malcolm."

The man takes hold of his girl's hand, "Get some things, you're staying at the ranch."

San Antonio

Micky storms into his office and barks at his nephew, "Move!"

Stoner rolls the office chair to the left leaving enough room for Micky to get into the desk drawer that holds his hooch. The way-too-sober PI pulls a long belt, then another, then another. "Fuckin bitch. Fuckin Price. You'd better get some shit on him, Stoner."

"Malcolm Price has an LLC called Lewis Burg," Stoner laughs. Sort of.

"What's the fucking joke?"

"Price is from Lewisburg, Pennsylvania. Lewis Burg. The LLC was formed in Texas in 2003 when the b-baller signed with the Spurs."

The private dick starts twitching. When that happens Micky knows he's on to something—or he's way too sober. "Keep digging, Stoner. I'll be at Paula's on the Chase, then at the arena."

"Diving," Stoner corrects.

"What the fuck is diving?"

"You don't dig in cyberspace, Micky. You dive."

"Shut the fuck up."

Stoner waits until Micky drives away, then lights a blunt. "No effing way I'm going back into Price's cyberspace. I went deep, maybe too deep on him already. That dive **had** to have caught the eye of someone at FICA. Don't want the cyber agents on my tail – might have put them there already, but if I don't go back..." He takes a seat, puts his laptop on Micky's desk, pulls up the stored file he created for The Malcolm Price and reviews the information he got from his prolonged hack. "I'll give this shit to

Micky, but not until he pushes for more. Until then, I'm staying the eff out of cyberland."

Washington, DC
FICA Agent, Kristen Millie, quadrant manager of the hacker-for-hire division at the Federal Investigative Cyber Agency, has been pouring over field reports from San Antonio, Texas, and Phoenix, Arizona. Both cities are part of Kristen's territory and both cities are part of this year's NBA Championship series. As is the way of things at FICA, the agents get busy when cyber hackers get busy, and they get busy when the spotlight shines extra bright on athletes, entertainers, and politicians.

On any given day, in any given month, the glorified and rarified are hounded by the press, and snooped on in the deep. But during playoff seasons, the weeks preceding award ceremonies, and throughout the political process, there is a noted uptick in hacking attempts on the participants of those events. A good percentage of cyber divers want the thrill of taking a peek-see into the lives of the rich and famous. They are classified as titillation divers. They don't do much more than get into a celeb's cyberspace, get out, and brag to their friends about getting in and getting out. The other percentage of divers, the ones who are classified as hackers, have more nefarious reasons for diving deep, and they are the ones who raise red flags and warrant surveillance. One such diver has caught the attention of Agent Millie and she has been waiting outside the office of FICA Director, Roland Gaffney, to discuss a red flag dive.

"You can go in, Agent."

Kristen pulls a deep breath and steadies her hand before entering. She hates that the director intimidates her, but he intimidates the hell out of her. She steps inside and remains at the door, he points to a seat, she sits. So as not to be staring at him as he finishes the call he ought to have finished before summoning her in, the agent scans his office and gets lost in thought.

"Agent Millie! I don't have all day. What have you got?"

She stands and pulls the files from under her arm, nearly dropping the damn lot of them. She quickly composes herself, "There's been a deep dive on 77."

"How deep?"

"A sustained look at his files: financials, professional and personal contracts, emails, and phone numbers were of particular interest to the hacker, and there was a deep dive into his LLC."

"Any idea who the diver is?"

"We're narrowing in, sir. My question is whether we should notify Mr. Price."

"Because of the playoffs?"

"Yes, Director."

"Hold off on notification. Put extra eyes on his cyberspace. If anyone becomes too interested or goes too deep, contact Price."

"Yes, sir."

AT&T Center

77 takes center court ready for blood, Utah Jazz blood. He knows the dick is in his regular seat, but he hasn't looked that way. Jason and a shitload of security have eyes on him, so all Malcolm needs to do is IT. He does IT and then some. After the win, Malcolm waits outside the meet and greet for Jason.

"Where's the dick?"

"Out in the parking lot with his car idling. He's going to follow you, so don't drive north. The detail is behind Micky's Lincoln, they'll follow the two of you and take care of the bastard when you stop to eat. I'm going back to the ranch, I don't want to leave Sage and Sammi alone."

Malcolm nods then opens the door to a thunderous chorus of, "77, 77, 77…" to which he replies, **"Is In The House!"**

The crowd goes wild. Malcolm's thoughts go to Sage.

Heading the Wrong Way

Micky Strong follows Malcolm Price to a roadside burger joint—somewhere between

San Antonio and Corpus Christi. The security detail follows Micky and while 77 is inside thrilling the diners and ordering a burger and fries to go, the security detail is doing a little obedience training with the pit bull. Malcolm waves to Micky when he pulls his Mercedes onto the road, opens her up, and heads to his Alamo Heights condo. He is finishing his burger and fries on his balcony when Micky barrel-asses his Lincoln to a screeching stop across the street. Malcolm lifts his feet off the railing, stands tall, and sends another wave to the dick.

The turning point.

Stoner pulls up short when he finds a prone Micky on the vinyl couch in the PI office just before noon. He taps his uncle's foot, "You drunk or dead?" He drops his backpack onto a chair and steps close, "Fuck, Micky, groan or something." When there's no response, Stoner gives his uncle's shoulders a shake and is sort of rewarded with a guttural moan and a hacking cough, "Shit. Do you need an ambulance?"

Micky pushes himself up, falls flat and tries again, "77 is dead..."

"Fuck, Micky, you killed Malcolm Price!?"

The pissed PI gets to a sitting position, "Not yet."

"Did he bust you up?"

Micky shakes his head and runs a hand through his hair, "Get my hooch and a paper towel." He winces when he presses a whiskey-wet wad to his busted lip, then holds his ribs tight when he starts coughing. "Price doesn't have the balls. His muscle worked me over."

"Shit, Micky. This grudge with Price is getting out of hand. Ain't no woman alive worth this crap."

"When I find that whore, she's gonna pay for the both of them."

Stoner grabs his backpack and starts for the door.

"Where the fuck you going?" The PI pauses. The PI thinks. The PI knows. "You found something on Price."

"Micky you should…"

"Stoner. Give him the fuck up."

The hacker, who is in way over his head, opens the door then pauses. "Price owns a ranch in Wyldwood, the old McCaid spread. He works with a real estate agent named Sammi Wilcox. She put the ranch purchase through Lewis Burg LLC as a blind sale." He pauses, wishes he could get out of this mess, but knows he can't. "Wilcox recently rented a place in Wyldwood the same way. The place could be for her, but…"

Micky laughs then coughs up some blood. "But it's for my whore."

I could just stay here forever.

It's been nearly two weeks since the parking lot incident and Micky hasn't been seen anywhere—not at his place, not at his hole-in-the-wall office, not at Paula's on the Chase, or at any of his usual haunts. He and his big-ass Lincoln dropped off the big-ass face of the world. The longer he stays underground, the more unsettled the people living at Wyldwood Ranch become. Worry intensifies further when Luke Haynes finds some trampling of crops in one of the fields and calls his supervisor. "Jason."

"What's up, Luke?"

"Looks like we had an intruder near the lower 40. He made it a good ways toward the shallow waters on the west end, then backtracked."

"Those fields are the easiest to access from the road. Are you thinking it's someone unfamiliar with the place?"

"Could be, but my gut is that it's someone who knows the lay of the land."

"Yeah? Any thoughts on that subject, Luke?"

"I had to let Hunt Mayfield go last week. He might be on a bender and looking for some trouble."

"Check it out and let me know. Get two of your men on that part of the spread overnight until further notice."

Sage goes under watch 24-7. If she isn't with Malcolm, she's with Jason and Sammi, or with Luke, but she's no longer allowed in the fields working the vegetation. She is allowed her riding time with Sammi so long as they stay on the frontend of the property or as close to the river run as possible.

"You've made real progress, Sage," Sammi opines as they make their way to the stables.

"I'm feeling right in the saddle now. I just love it, Sammi."

"We'll see how much lovin' there is after you tack your own ride from now on."

"Will I be riding Philbert, today?"

"Should hope so considering he's yours, now."

Sage stops cold, "He is?"

"He is. You can ride others, too..."

Sage rushes past Sammi, calling over her shoulder, "No thanks. I can't wait to ride MY boy."

Sammi finds Sage rubbing and nuzzling Philbert's nose. "Here," she says as she hands her a lead.

Sage reaches under her horse's neck, hooks the lead, opens the stall, walks Philbert a bit, attaches the lead to a wall, grabs another that's hanging from an opposing wall and attaches it to Philbert. All the while, she's talking to her boy, "Now go easy on me. I'm new at this."

"You're off to a good start, Sage. You, too, Philbert."

Sage leans in and whispers, "You're such a good boy."

The "good boy" gives a couple nods of his head and a wet snort.

Sammi interrupts playtime and gets down to business. "Before you saddle your horse, you need to groom your horse's back and girth. Grit, burrs, and debris can become lodged in your horse's coat and if you don't remove it, it can lead to chaffing or discomfort that can make your horse misbehave."

While Sammi talks, Sage grabs hold of a brush and starts in.

"Okay. Nice work. Now we're going to check Philbert's hooves. You need to do this before every ride. You look for anything that might be lodged in – I'll do some cleaning and checking for things like thrush, or any looseness in the shoes. Good. Now grab the pads and blanket. Check them for any debris that can cause discomfort. Make sure when you put the blanket onto the pad both are nice and smooth. I did a tack check earlier, but you'll always want to check the saddle for frayed stitching, or cracked leather, anything that might show wear or tear. Rings, buckles, and bits need to be checked for sharp edges. We'll go over all of that during the next few days of tacking. Basically, you'll do all of this because you won't have a comfortable ride if your horse is uncomfortable."

Sage gives Philbert a scratch between the ears. "How are we doing, boy?"

He gives her a couple head bobs and another snort.

She gives him a nuzzle and a big laugh.

Sammi joins in, "Well, Malcolm sure chose the right horse for you."

Sage beams.

The rest of the lesson goes smoothly, as does the ride. Sammi leads along the river to the west end then leads them through shallow waters. When they reach the backend she brings the trot to a cantor – the cantor to a gallop. Sage follows suit. They ride to a small hill, dismount, and sit beneath a grove of trees.

"I think this my favorite place on the ranch. Nope. I think it's my favorite place in the whole world. I could just stay here forever."

"Well, you'll be staying at the ranch until Micky's found, that's for sure. And we can ride here every day if you want."

Sage offers a smile, but her words tell what she's really thinking. "Micky won't ever give up on finding me, Sammi."

"Are you sure? I mean you were only with him a short time."

"I wasn't **with** him at all. That's the problem. He bought and paid for me, so in his mind he owns me." Sage leans back against the tree that's offering them shade and offers a reflection. "Some would say Malcolm owns me, too."

Sammi begins a response, but is cut off.

"I couldn't argue that point, but I'd certainly add to it."

"How's that?"

"I'd say Malcolm owns my heart."

Too far off the mark.

Malcolm is carrying the weight of Sage and Micky, and the weight of the playoffs — he is not carrying **any** of it well. "Where the fuck is Micky?" he snaps.

Unfamiliar with the tone, Jason wades in. "Don't know. He hasn't been seen since the security detail handled him in the parking lot."

"Any chance he's dead?"

"No."

"Any chance he's seeing things differently?"

"No. The security guys are staking out his place and his stomping grounds, Malcolm, but that's all we can do right now. Unless…"

The boss pushes back before his employee finishes. "No cops. Not yet. Wyldwood law knows I've got a woman with me. If Micky ever shows up we'll get them involved, but the dick is from San Antonio. If I report him to the cops down there, they won't give a shit about protecting my privacy. They'll get up in my shit and the life I've built in Wyldwood will go to shit. Besides, they won't do a damned thing to protect Sage. We have to handle this, Jason." Malcom thinks a minute, "Micky's not coming to the games, but you know damn well he's still playing the bookies. Follow the money."

"On it, Malcolm."

"And tell Sage I'll be back at Wyldwood, tonight."

Too close for comfort.

Micky Strong watches from a feed store parking lot on the thoroughfare in Wyldwood as a black Mercedes heads toward the ranch. The excited dick places a call to Stoner. "I'll be damned. My fuckup nephew knows a thing or two about computers."

"Is that supposed to be a compliment, Uncle Asshole?"

Micky laughs. "I won't beat your head in for that one, but only because you got it right when you said Lewis Burg LLC is tied to Malcolm Price and the realtor bitch is on his payroll. Sammi Wilcox is big shit in the ranch selling business, so I'm banking she might be in the rent-a-whore-an-apartment business too. Find out where that rental is."

"It'll cost you."

"Always does."

The PI doesn't need to follow Price to the ranch; he's already been by the main entrance a few times—already knows that he can't get onto it from the frontend or the backend. "I'll just have to wait until the bitch comes out of hiding or Stoner finds something more on Sammi Wilcox. It's just a matter of time, and I've got Time. To. Kill."

Micky pulls onto the thoroughfare with a new game plan. "Don't want the bitch or the fucking brat baby—I want to make **Malcolm** pay the fucking **Price** for the rest of his fucking life." He laughs all the way back to San Antonio.

What's the yearly thing?

Conference play closes with the Spurs headed to the NBA Finals for the third time in three years — **The Malcolm Price** years as they are being touted, on and off the airwaves. A monumental accomplishment for the 25-year-old b-baller, for sure, but the upcoming toe to toe scuffle between LeBron James and Malcolm Price — the 1st and 28th round picks in the 2003 NBA draft, has whipped the sports world into a frenzy.

The residents of Wyldwood Ranch aren't swept into that swirl because they are gripped by the uncertainty surrounding Micky Strong.

The Box
A big-ass Lincoln is parked outside a storage unit in the blighted Eastgate section of San Antonio. Micky has been inside the box for days, kicked back in a slack-ass recliner with an industrial-size fan blowing hot, recycled air his way. He pulls a gun from a side pocket on the chair at the sound of a car pulling up outside. He puts it back when Stoner wraps on the door.

"You wanted to see me?" he asks as he rolls up the box door.

"Yeah. Sit down. Shut up."

Stoner starts to say some shit, but when he sees the look on Micky's face, he sits down and shuts up.

"I have a few things to tie up, then I'm leaving this fuckin' state. You're gonna do three things for me before I leave, and at least one thing every year after that. One: give me the keys to your car. I'm using it until I'm done with business. I'll let you know when and where to pick it up. Two: I want you to take the Lincoln to some hick-ass corner of this big-ass state and torch it. Get rid of the VIN number before you blaze it. Don't fuck this up, Stoner. Three: keep the rental on this place paid in full and on time. I'll be leaving a few things behind and I want them to be here if I come back for them."

"What's the yearly thing?"

"I'll let you know." Micky pulls an envelope from the recliner's side pocket, "Here."

Stoner's eyes grow wide, "Shit. Must be..."

"Ten grand. There'll be 5Gs for the yearly work. DO NOT put one cent of that money or any money I pay you in a bank. Look, Stoner, the money you made for my PI work shouldn't cause you much trouble, but the hacking on Price might cause you some heat. If you get busted, keep your mouth shut. You might do a few years in some minimum-security joint if they can track your hacking efforts to me, but there'll be a payday waiting on you. If you've got records or shit about Price, get rid of them. As for the money in your pocket — that can be traced to me and if you get caught with it, it will put you behind bars for years. Understood?"

"Understood."

The uncle and nephew trade keys and an awkward hug, "Now, get out, and don't be stupid."

Wyldwood

The weekend leading to the Finals starts off easy for Malcolm and Sage. When he isn't pounding the practice floor at the Center, he's with her, in whatever creative ways they can be. She's been taking birth control for weeks, counting every damn dose and dithering on and on about the wait for their first time together.

"I swear, Malcolm, this package of pills is never ending. Maybe I should double up or something."

"Follow the directions, Sage."

"I need to feel you. All of you," she sighs.

"Relax, Girl, once I start burying it deep, it'll stay put."

77 is heading off ranch Sunday morning and won't return until after the Finals. He spends all of his time Saturday with Sage— some of it outdoors walking the ranch and riding the trails.

"You're looking good in that saddle, Girl."

She smiles over her shoulder, "I suspect Philbert will be my second favorite ride on this ranch."

"Damn straight," he gallops past her.

When she meets up with him at the stables, she shakes her head at the ranch hand, "Thank you, but Mr. Price and I will handle this."

"Handle what?"

"Your horse – your responsibility. Tend to your horse, Mr. Price."

"I'm not sure I'm liking this pushy side, Girl."

"Deal."

Malcolm laughs big.

They spend a bit more time walking and talking. "This is the prettiest place I've ever seen, Malcolm. Of course I'm from Tucks, so not much in the way of comparison, but I'd say this land is perfect."

"You still like Garden Oasis?"

"Second prettiest place in the whole world! The garden terrace is full of blooms and I was working with Luke the other day and he told me some real interesting things. Did you know the little yellow trumpet flowers that cover the white picket fence are called Carolina Jessamine, or Gelsemium sempervirens, and they are toxic through and through with strychnine or arsenic, or I don't know, but they're real poisonous. Can you believe that something so beautiful can be so deadly?"

Malcolm brushes Sage's bangs and pulls long strands of her hair through his fingers. He locks onto her eyes and looks deep, "I can believe it." They stop at a fence where Malcolm lifts Sage onto the top rail... "Girl, do you have plans?"

"Plans?"

"Do you want to work, go to school, anything?"

"May I? Go to school? I'd love to get my GED, maybe take online courses in horticulture."

"Do it, Girl. Tell Sammi what you need. Anything else?"

Sage shrugs.

Malcolm senses a hesitancy—he doesn't like it, "Girl?"

Sage pulls an unsteady breath, "I need a place for Momma. A resting place."

"At the ranch?" he asks, but it sounds more like a suggestion.

Tears fill her eyes. They hold tight as she points to a tiny hill with a grove of trees, "Right there is lovely."

"Let's do it." Malcolm wipes a single tear from Sage's lash. "Come on, let's go get your momma."

Micky Strong gets hard when he sees Sage in the passenger seat of the Mercedes that purrs by. He puts Stoner's shit box Camry in gear and follows Price's car until it turns onto a pebble path off of the main thoroughfare. "So that's where the damned turnoff is," Micky growls. "Once again, Stoner, delivers." Micky drives past the little road and waits at the feed store up the street. An hour later the Mercedes pulls onto the thoroughfare and heads back toward the ranch.

Micky inches the Camry down the pebble path and stops when he comes upon a fairytale cottage surrounded by a white picket fence covered in yellow flowers. "Bingo." He gets out of the car and walks the property, "Well, isn't this the cutest little whorehouse in Texas?" he laughs. The PI drives back to the feed store, leaves the Camry, and hoofs it down the thoroughfare until he reaches a treed area that abuts the property. He ducks into the tree line and moves inward toward the cottage. It takes a couple of minutes, but he eventually pushes through, exiting just opposite a fieldstone path leading to a garden room off the back of Oasis. "This will work." Micky backtracks, gets into Stoner's car, and gets the fuck out of Wyldwood. By the time he arrives back in San Antonio, he has a purpose and a plan, "Grab the hundred grand from the storage facility, put half on the Spurs, wait until Malcolm Price makes me bank, kill the bitch and the kid—then fucking crush Malcolm Price for the rest of his fucking life."

He grabs his cell and calls the escort service, "Eve, it's Micky, I need a piece of ass to sit next to me at the Center. Get me a blonde with big tits this time."

Welcome to the 2007
NBA Championship
Finals

      Malcolm glances at section 109 when he takes center court. Micky Strong is on his feet and at his regular seat, his arm slung over the shoulder of a buxom blonde. The dick sends a smile and a wave 77's way. It sets the point guard Off – His – Game. His team pays the price going down by twenty-two points at the halftime buzzer. When the Spurs return to the boards, 77 gets his head off the dick and onto the court. Before the player turns IT around, the crowd's chants of "77" take on an angry, edgy tone. The fans push past the MAN and side with their team with chants of "Go Spurs Go!" That sets the point guard straight. He pushes against the vitriol, steps it up, and answers the call. Grit and luck lead the Spurs to a low-scoring victory over the Cavs.

Game Two

Micky is back with Blondie, and 77 is back in fighting form. The Spurs go up two games over the Cavs, winning by eleven points.

Game Three

Malcolm loses IT at practice, and is unable to find IT during the game. He hands the Cavs the edge and a sizeable lead before putting some fight into his game. The Spurs grunt their way to a three point win at the buzzer.

Game Four

The Malcolm Price is against the wall. His focus is gone – his tempo is off – his patience is thin – and his temper is shot to shit. One more penalty and he is out of the game. He sprints to the sideline, takes a seat and works on settling himself. Something in the stands catches his eye—someone in the stands catches his eye. A tall, distinguished man in jeans and tweed sport coat is leaning against a wall, his feet crossed at the ankles, his eyes drilling 77. The man nods. The buzzer breaks Malcolm's stare and calls him back to the game. His game. The one he refuses to lose.

The last three minutes of play are ugly, but his **team** wins the Title by one point.

The angry player heads to the meet and greet after he makes a call to Sage. "Girl, be in my bed when I get home. I'm burying deep, so deal."

Wyldwood

Sage hears the purr of the Mercedes, goes to the window and pulls back a lace curtain.

Malcolm catches movement above him and sees his girl's nakedness backlit by soft flickering lights. He tears up the porch stairs, through the foyer, and to the second floor balcony-wrap in seconds. He pushes the bedroom door almost off its hinges.

Sage is still at the window, the moon backlighting her now. Candles of every shape and size flicker in the room. "Congratulations," she whispers.

"Don't." Malcolm crosses to her. "No words."

He strips, presses her against the wall, and pushes in. He ignores her whimper. He knows he should ease up, but he needs her. He needs to get into her and out of his head. He ignores her second whimper.

Sage pushes against him. "You said I'm not your whore, Malcolm. You're hurting me."

He eases up and lets her pull herself free. Sage tries to step around him. He takes hold of her wrist to stop her, leans her back against the wall again, "Sage," he lifts her into his arms. "I'm sorry. I'm sorry. Lay with me, Girl. I'll do you right." Malcolm places her on the bed, works her tenderly — then buries himself deep.

Malcolm Price got out of his head—
Sage Finley got into his heart.

The lovers lock themselves behind closed doors for nearly a week. They laugh and love as though they've been together, always. The night before Malcolm heads out of town for a publicity tour, Sage flutters from the bathroom in a frothy, ruffled, sexy little number. She is busily rubbing cream over her arms and shoulders.

Malcolm responds favorably to the outfit and the rubbing, "Come here, I want to taste you."

Sage climbs on top and kisses him.

Malcolm flips her, "Not the taste I want, Girl."

She giggles until she can't pull air.

The pro-baller leaves at the end of June, television appearances, press junkets, magazine interviews, the whole works. On his way out of town, he drops Sage at the cottage. "Sammi and Jason will be by. Let them spend time with you here. You can tend to your flowers, whatever, but make sure you sleep at the ranch."

Sage kisses her man, "I will."

"Keep the door locked and the security on."

She does as she is told.

Planning their lives.

When 77 returns to the ranch, the young lovers make up for lost time. They are inseparable throughout the month of July and begin talking about the future. Sage gets her GED score, sends an application to A&M, and selects online horticultural courses for the fall. Malcolm makes secret plans with Jason and Sammi to move her to the ranch when he returns from an upcoming trip to Lewisburg. Together, the young couple plans a September 3rd burial ceremony for her momma's ashes on the tiny hill beneath the grove of trees. Sage answers Malcolm's unasked question, "September 3rd is Momma's birthday, her thirty-fifth birthday."

Planning her death.

Micky Strong spends the month of July taking care of business. He cashed in big time with the bookies, courtesy of the Spurs sweep of the Finals. He closes his PI office, pays off his lease agreement on his apartment, buys a new identity, and a brand-spanking-new 12-inch blade. Micky tosses Stoner another five grand, "Find out when Malcolm Price is gonna be out of town."

Stoner **should** think twice about this request – really, he should think twice about this request. He doesn't. The hacker figures the work is just a tap and grab, a shallow dive into Price's shit, nothing that will raise any red flags with FICA. He goes in, gets the information in a matter of minutes, and gets the fuck out. He reports his findings to his uncle. "77 is going to his hometown on August first for a citywide celebration of their local legend. He'll be back in Texas on the fifth."

"What time?"

"Arriving at Austin-Bergstrom at 9:15 PM."

"That puts him back in Wyldwood around 10. Perfect."

I'll be back on the fifth.

"Grab whatever you need for a few days, you and I are staying at Oasis until I head to Pennsylvania."

"Really?" she squeals. "You've never stayed the night there. Why are…"

"Girl, grab your stuff and let's go."

As soon as Malcolm's taillights fade, Sammi and Jason set about rearranging things at the ranch. They move some of Sage's things from Mama Girl's room to the master suite, leaving just enough behind so she's none the wiser. Then they set about turning the room next to Malcolm's study into one for Sage. They follow Malcolm's instructions to the letter, but Sammi adds a significant touch of her own.

"Set it up there, Jason."

"Bold move, Sammi. Not sure how the boss is gonna take to this."

"When he sees the look on Sage's face, he'll be thanking me."

Before leaving the study, Jason and Sammi relax a bit in front of Sage's very own electric fireplace. Jason leans in and nudges his woman, "I think both of them will be thanking you rightly, Miss Sammi Wilcox."

Malcolm pulls Sage close and holds her tight. "I'll be back on the fifth. You can stay at Oasis during the day, but make sure Luke or Sammi or Jason are nearby. Security will do check-ins with you if you're alone and if they tell you to go to the ranch, make sure you go. Don't stay here at night, Sage."

"Except on the fifth, right? I can wait here for you to get back from Lewisburg, right?"

"Right."

"Because you have a surprise for me at the ranch, right?"

"Right." He pulls her close again, "Now lock up and put on security."

She does as she is told.

Philly
Damian Johnson meets his best friend at the VIP lounge at Philadelphia International Airport. After a best friend hug, and a round of, "How the hell are you ….. you're sure looking good ….. damn it's good to see you," the men head to Damian's ride.

Malcolm laughs big, "A cop car? I sort of wanted to sneak my way into Lewisburg. Not much chance of that with you behind the wheel of this, Sergeant Johnson."

Damian laughs big, "I've five things to say on that subject, Mr. Price."

"I'm sure you have."

"Penn Valley, Danville, Sunbury, Northumberland County, and Bloomsburg Municipal. I'd say they are all fine airports and they are minutes from Lewisburg, and let's not forget number six…"

"Fox Hollow," Malcolm laughs.

"So you **do** remember that Fox Hollow airport is located within the borough of Lewisburg. Now, since you dragged my ass across the Keystone State, you're gonna sit back and keep still while I make our presence known."

"Fine, but don't turn on the lights and siren until we're on the Interstate."

"Deal. I figure that ought to give you enough time to tell me about your girl."

"Mama Girl's been flapping her jaws, I see."

"She has. Now it's your turn."

Malcolm remains silent for quite a bit. "Sage has taken up some space in my heart, Damian."

"I can see that. What about your plan?"

"To do my pro-ball years alone. That plan?"

Damian nods.

"Sage blew that plan to shit."

"You gonna take a knee for the girl?"

"Not thinking about knees, Damian. I'm too damned busy trying to keep her alive. There's this guy who's after her."

"Are the cops involved?"

"Not yet."

Damian puts on the lights and sirens, "They are now. Let's get home and make a plan to keep your girl safe."

The best evening, ever!

Sage spends the morning of August fifth with Luke, pruning this and trimming that. She tells him about a rare Blue Evening Primrose bush she wants to start from seeds, nurture in the garden terrace, and eventually plant outside. "They are perfectly beautiful," she gushes. "The vibrant blue petals are trimmed in white, just as though they've been painted by hand, and the center is the bright yellow of the Lone Star. I want the Blue Evenings to be my addition to this beautiful landscape."

After the gardener leaves, Sage moves about the cottage, trying to get out a belly full of nervous energy. She dusts, vacuums, changes bed linens, scours the bathroom and kitchen, and spends hours tending to her garden, but she's still wound tight. She plops onto the bed with her cell and scrolls through a series of pictures she took of her time with Malcolm on their walkabouts at the ranch, chooses her favorite shot, prints it, trims it to fit, and puts it into the black picture frame in the bedroom. She takes the picture of 'Jessica and Alex' and tucks it inside the drawer for safe keeping. "You've been so kind to keep me company at this beautiful Oasis," she laughs big.

Mid-afternoon, Sammi and Jason stop by to check in and have lunch. The man who's come to think of Sage as a kid sister is relieved to find she had the door locked and the security on when they arrived. "Listen Sage, Micky is still in the wind. No one has seen him since the Finals. His bookies said he made a killing off of the Spurs, and soon after he closed his business and gave up his apartment. We don't know what that means or where he is."

"Do you think he's gone? Do you think this is over?"

"Don't know what to think, but we need to act as though he's still a threat. I talked to Malcolm earlier. He said you're waiting here for him, then coming to the ranch. What's the plan for the rest of the day?"

"I got my curriculum for the online courses at A&M, and some of the work is already posted in the portal. I thought I'd do some of the assignments before Malcolm gets back. By the way, Jason, what's a portal?"

"Come on, I'll show you."

Jason and Sammi skip out a little after 7 PM. He calls over of his shoulder, "The detail will be by to check on things at 8 and 9. Lock up and put the security on."

She does as she is told.

The increasingly excited young woman can barely wait until 10 PM. She spends time reading her coursework and getting a jump start on a few assignments. At 8 PM she answers a call from security saying they are approaching the cottage. She steps out onto the front porch for a bit of fresh air while they are doing their property check, "Thanks, guys."

"Everything looks good, Ms. Finley. We'll be back by at 9."

"And Malcolm will be back at 10!" she squeals and happy two-steps.

"Please step back inside and lock up."

"Will do. Bye."

Micky watches from the tree line.

Sage works a bit more at her computer then heads for a bubble bath. At 9 PM she answers the security call from the comforts of her tub, "Hi guys."

"Everything set, Ms. Finley?"

"All set. Thanks."

"Have a good evening."

"I think tonight will be the best evening ever!"

Sufficiently unwound, Sage gets out of the tub, dries off, and slips into a tank top and pair of boy short bottoms. She straightens the bed, and puts on the electric fireplace. "Maybe

Malcolm will want to crash here after his long trip." She goes to her vanity, pulls her waist-length hair into a high ponytail and dabs a bit of perfume on her wrists and along her neck. She makes her way to the living room sofa, drags a heavy textbook onto her lap and starts reading about the germination process of wildflowers. Two chapters in, she falls into a deep sleep.

A knock on the front door drags her from her dreams. She keys the security pad, pulls open the door, and sees the twelve-inch blade a second before it finds her.

I should have...

Sage Finley is sprawled on the floor; her body is half in, half out of her garden cottage in an ever-spreading pool of blood. Her eyes are locked onto clay pots full of beautiful flowers. Colorful little innocents that sit in stark contrast to the shiny wet crimson splatter that runs the length of walls and soaks into the cushions of overturned furniture she banged against in her attempt to flee – to live.

The slumbering young woman unlocked and opened her door without asking who was on the other side. "I'm coming," she said when a knock pulled her from the couch, "I fell asleep and was having the most wonderful dream." Sage had been warned about the door...

"Keep the door locked, the security on, and don't open the door to anyone but me ... don't open the door to anyone ... don't open ..."

The beautiful young woman with the wide toothy smile and happy future ahead heeded those warnings before – but she had fallen asleep – and she forgot – and she was expecting her man at the door – the man who rescued her – and loved her — not the one who burst in and began savagely raging her. Tiny flashes of light and odd clicking sounds filled the last bits of her consciousness. As she struggled to stay on this side of life, Sage Finley watched Micky Strong casually walk out of the French doors of her terrace. A warm August breeze moved through those open doors, found her and lovingly caressed her.

Malcolm...is that you...Momma

Sage Finley's last words may have passed her lips or drifted as a thought. They most definitely moved in concert with her eyes as they fixed and dilated upon the clay pots full of beautiful flowers she lovingly tended to that afternoon.

I shouldn't have...

Malcolm inches toward the emergency vehicles stationed along the thoroughfare at the end of the pebble path. He stops next to a local deputy, "What happened, Billy?" He forces himself to ask, though he already knows.

The young man shakes his head, "A young woman .... a young woman was murdered in her little cottage, Mr. Price. I'm **so sorry**, Mr. Price."

"How?" Malcolm chokes.

"Stabbing. It must have been someone she knew. Someone raged that girl to death."

Malcolm hears the word "girl" and loses it.

Micky Strong

All shit breaks loose in The Lone Star state. Before Sage's blood has dried on the floor and walls of Garden Oasis, rumors start swirling that she was a paid escort of 77. Folks in Wyldwood suspect that's the case, but not a single one of them says a damn word to the flock of reporters that line the thoroughfare waiting for a glimpse of The Malcolm Price — an unlikely event given that he disappeared after learning about Sage and hasn't been seen or heard from since.

Local law enforcement, who have never worked a case like this rise to the occasion and are quick to establish an airtight alibi for Malcolm Price in part because of a courtesy call from Sergeant Damian Johnson of Lewisburg, PA.

"Thanks for calling in, Sergeant. We've locked down Mr. Price's timeline for August 5 and the days preceding, so you can rest some that our focus isn't on him, but it sure would help if…"

"…you knew where he currently is," Damian finishes the sentence.

"Yes, Sergeant. We're starting to feel the heat from investigators over in Bastrop County and some ugliness is wafting our way from down south. There's enough to keep San Antonio detectives busy with the whereabouts of Micky Strong, but…"

"…they're gonna start digging to see if Malcolm had someone deal with Micky."

"Yes, Sergeant. If you're in touch with Mr. Price, you need to encourage him to come back to Wyldwood and talk to us while he still has the chance."

"Thank you, Sheriff."

By sunset that day, Sheriff Stan Scarborough, and his son, Deputy Billy Scarborough, had worked a timeline for the people who spent the last hours with Sage and they've called them in for questioning. "Luke Haynes, come on in," the sheriff says to the man he's known for the better part of five decades. "What's your story, Luke?"

"I spent the morning with Ms. Finley at Garden Oasis tending the outdoor foliage."

"And her spirits?"

"Happy. She was looking forward to Mr. Price's return from Pennsylvania, and going on about introducing Blue Evening Primrose bushes into her gardens," Luke's voice cracks as he puts his arms onto his knees and hangs his head.

The sheriff gives him a minute then, "Any idea who killed Sage Finley?"

"Micky Strong."

The sheriff walks Luke out. "Sammi Wilcox, you're next. Have a seat. What's your story, Sammi?"

"Jason and I spent the afternoon with Sage at Garden Oasis. We had lunch mid-afternoon, shot the breeze for a while, then she planned to do some coursework from A&M."

"Coursework?"

"She was starting school there in the fall. Well, she was doing her coursework online, but she was over the moon about studying horticulture. She said there were some assignments already listed in an online portal that she needed help accessing, so Jason walked her through it." There is a noticeable pause and a rush of tears.

"When you're ready, Sammi."

"Sorry, Stan – I mean Sheriff Scarborough. It's just that Sage was so happy yesterday, and now she's."

Stan pushes in. "After Jason helped Ms. Finley with her computer work, you and Jason..."

"We got ready to leave. Jason cautioned her about keeping the place locked, said Wyldwood security would be making a swing by Oasis at 8 and 9 PM, and that she should expect Malcolm by 10 PM."

"Why did Jason caution Ms. Finley about keeping the place locked – why was there a security team checking on her?"

Sammi pushes out a breath and shakes her head.

"Sammi, who do you think killed Sage Finley?"

"Micky Strong."

The sheriff walks Sammi out. "Jason Carpenter, you're next. Have a seat. Tell me **the what fuck** about Sage Finley and a paid security detail. I don't suspect you'll tell me everything until you talk to your boss, but you'd better tell me enough if you want to keep the flames that are already flaring from burning his ass."

"Micky Strong, a private dick from San Antonio made good on his promise to get Sage Finley back for leaving him for Malcolm Price. My men and I tried to keep her safe and we fucking failed. That's all you're getting from me, Sheriff."

Luke, Sammi, and Jason are ruled out as suspects. Wyldwood security personnel turn over their records, and help canvass people along the thoroughfare. It is confirmed that Micky Strong had been in Wyldwood on and off for weeks, but no one can attest to seeing him on the day of the murder. When Sheriff Scarborough contacts San Antonio requesting information about the PI, he learns there's an investigation already underway into the disappearance of Micky Strong — and another one into the disappearance of Malcolm Price. Then he is put on notice.

"The sharing of information, Sheriff Scarborough, hinges on the sharing of witnesses for statements," Detective Romney of the San Antonio Police Department snarls.

Asked and answered.

Sammi Wilcox

The friend of Sage Finley and loyalist of Malcolm Price is the first person brought to San Antonio for questioning. She is immediately put on notice by the detective, "We're gonna talk about the hooker who was living in a rental property listed under your name, Ms. Wilcox."

Sammi waits for more.

"You work for Malcolm Price. Is that correct?"

"When he has real estate needs, yes. Mr. Price bought the McCaid spread through me."

"Yes, and rented his secret hideaway for hookers from you."

Sammi keeps her mouth. Barely.

"You live on Mr. Price's ranch with his ranch hand, Jason Carpenter."

It wasn't a question, but she answered it anyway. "Yes."

"Garden Oasis is owned by former Congressman Walter Pendleton and his wife, Mavis."

"Yes."

"We contacted them in Florida. They said you recently handled the rental of their property, but they didn't know much about the whore living there."

Sammi bites her tongue. Hard.

"If you live at Wyldwood Ranch with Jason Carpenter. Why did you rent Garden Oasis?"

"I rented it for Sage Finley."

"Why?"

"I was trying to help her get out of her circumstances."

"You mean the escort business?"

"Yes."

"Why would you want to help this hooker?"

Sammi cringes at the detective's insistence. "Because Mr. Price asked me to."

"Why?"

"You'll have to ask Mr. Price, Detective."

"You can bet your sweet ass I will, Ms. Wilcox, just as soon as I find him."

Jason Carpenter

"Where's your boss?"

Jason shrugs.

"When was the last time you saw him?"

"August first."

"The day he headed home for a celebration in Lewisburg. Funny thing, Malcolm Price flew Austin to Philadelphia – that's hours by car from Lewisburg. Any idea why?"

Jason shrugs.

"When was the last time you heard from him?"

"August fifth."

"Explain."

"He called to confirm his return travel plans."

"You're the head of Wyldwood Ranch."

"Yes."

"You're the head of security at the ranch."

"Yes."

"You're Price's right-hand-man, the one who handles his ranch – and his security detail – and his problems."

Jason knows where this line of shit is heading. He waits it out.

"Micky Strong was a problem for Sage Finley – which means he was a problem for Malcolm Price. From what we've learned so far, Strong didn't like that his hooker left him for Price. Can't say I blame him, she was a beautiful girl. A paid escort, but still…"

Jason stands up. "Am I free to go?"

"You are."

Jason heads for the door, stops cold at the detective's final jab.

"Micky Strong most likely killed Sage Finley."

Jason turns and nods.

"Question now is whether the private dick is on the run or if he's dead? Makes me wonder if the right-hand-man of Malcolm Price handled another one of his **problems** while Price was conveniently out of town?"

Wendel "Stoner" Strong

"Where's Micky?"
"Don't know."
"Do you know anything about that?" the detective points.

Stoner picks up a piece of paper from the corner of the detective's desk and reads.

Federal Investigative Cyber Agency
Memorandum
Re: Malcolm Price
From: FICA Agent, Kristen Millie
Quadrant Manager: Hacker Division

Please be advised, FICA is investigating incidents of cyber hacking on the above-named subject during the months of: May 2007 and July 2007. Recent events in the Texas jurisdictions of Wyldwood and San Antonio suggest individuals associated with Class C Private Investigator, Micky Strong, may be questioned in the murder of Sage Finley.

Should Wendel "Stoner" Strong be brought in for questioning in matters unrelated to the cyber hacking of Malcolm Price, the FBI and FICA release investigative claim. If information pertaining to the above-referenced cyber hacking

of Malcolm Price is the byproduct of any criminal investigation, please desist further questioning and notify, FICA Agent, Kristen Millie.

Stoner tosses the paper onto Detective Romney's desk. "I'm outta here."

"Don't leave the state of Texas, Mr. Strong."

Malcolm Price

San Antonio detectives make a trip to Wyldwood at the end of August to speak with Malcolm Price.

"Did you know Sage Finley?"

"I did."

"Was she a paid escort?"

"She was."

"Was she a paid escort of yours?"

"No, she was not."

"When did you learn she was in that line of work?"

"At the beginning of the playoffs. Micky Strong, a private investigator in San Antonio, brought her to a Spurs meet and greet. She was his escort that night."

"And she ended up living near your ranch in Wyldwood. Care to explain?"

"No."

"Fine. Let me tell you what we know, Mr. Price." Detective Romney goes all-in. "**We know** Micky Strong introduced you to his working girl at a meet and greet. **We know** your right-hand-man, Jason Carpenter, invited them to the event at your request. **We know** Micky mouthed off that you took Sage Finley from him that night. **We know** you and the former hooker were the singular focus of the PI for months. **We know** Micky paid a hacker to get information on you. **We know** he found your secret ranch. **We know** he was seen up in Wyldwood prior to the murder of Ms. Finley. **We know** he left his life behind in July and hasn't been seen or heard from since August 5. **We know** Sage Finley was hacked to pieces in a sweet little cottage paid for by you. **And we know there is a lot more to this story**."

Malcolm gets up and points to the door, "This is what I know. Micky Strong killed Sage Finley. I know you are wasting my time. And I know that I am done." Malcolm addresses Jason, "Make sure you escort the detectives off my property."

A private goodbye.

On September 3rd, on a tiny hill beneath a grove of trees at Wyldwood Ranch, Malcolm Price buries the ashes of Sage Finley and her momma. He packs the fresh soil, places a single white rose tied with a sage ribbon onto their grave and walks away—without so much as a look back.

Reasons

Book 3

Malcolm Price

2008 ---

Welcome to the 2008
NBA Championship Series
Western Conference – First Round

"Have to tell you, Don, I didn't think Price would get the Spurs back into the playoffs this year..."

"...not many men could ignore the noise and the intrusion into their personal life like 77 has..."

"...and deliver the way he has..."

"...still, it remains to be seen if he can keep his head in the game."

Mavs sweeps Spurs
in First Round Play

Malcolm spends a week in San Antonio after his team's loss then heads to Wyldwood. His Mercedes idles a bit at the side of the thoroughfare before he turns off and travels the pebble path toward Garden Oasis. At his request, Sammi purchased the place outright from Walt and Mavis the month he buried Sage, but he hadn't been near the place since the night he left for Lewisburg. He parks his Mercedes along the picket fence and lets the memories of his time with Sage kick his ass...

"It's 77."

Sage opened the door.

The MAN was pushed back by her beauty, angered by other things.

Sage was dressed in the same outfit as earlier in the evening, but she was accessorized with a red grab mark on her bicep and a handprint across her face.

"Get your things," he said through clenched teeth.

She wagged her purse toward him, "This is it."

~

Malcolm reached across the car and placed his hand on the weeping girl's knee, "You're with me now."

She placed her hand on top of his and pushed her words through a bit of ugly crying. "I know you are trying to make a difference in my life, though I don't know why." She wrapped her fingers around his and gave a small squeeze. The corners of her lips turned upward as a final tear slid down her cheek, "I can't get out of my life, Malcolm. It's already heading for disaster. I couldn't afford Momma's medicine **and** my birth control; I chose Momma's medicine. I'm pregnant with Micky's kid." Sage let go of Malcolm's hand.

He pulled it back and gave it a tender squeeze, "What do you want to do, Sage?"

"I don't want it, but if I don't have it and Micky finds out, He. Will. Kill. Me."

"Then he doesn't find out."

~

"Come here. I want to taste you."

Sage walked the few steps to him, placed a foot on either side of his crossed feet and pressed against him. His excitement was long and hard along her belly. He skipped his fingertips across her bangs, then ran his hand the length of her long hair before cupping the back of her head. He kissed her long and deep, groaning long and deep. "I want to do things with you, Sage, but you're in no condition, and there are things about this arrangement you need to understand. You are not my whore. You have a say in what we do if we do. When you want out, you're out. There isn't a fairytale ending in this fairytale cottage. If you fall in love you will end up being hurt. Think about it when I'm gone."

~

She stirred when his fingers brushed away bangs from her forehead. She opened her eyes, shook her head, and closed them again.

"Come here, Girl."

Sage leaned into him. He wrapped her tight and let her cry.

"Mama Girl said you'll feel the loss," he whispered.

"Even though I didn't want it?" she asked through sobs.

"Even though." Malcolm held Sage until she fell back to sleep and until the next morning's light.

~

The weekend leading into the Finals started off easy for Malcolm and Sage. When he wasn't pounding the practice floor at the Center, he was with her in whatever creative ways they could be. She'd been taking birth control for weeks, counting every damn dose and dithering on and on about the wait for their first time together.

"I swear, Malcolm, this package of pills is never ending. Maybe I should double up or something."

"Follow the directions, Sage."

"I need to feel you. All of you," she sighed.

"Relax, Girl, once I start burying it deep, it'll stay put."

~

Sage heard the purr of the Mercedes move down the access road. She went to the window and pulled back a lace curtain.

Malcolm caught movement above him — saw his girl's nakedness backlit by soft flickering light. He tore up the porch stairs, through the foyer, and to the second floor balcony-wrap in seconds. He pushed the bedroom door almost off its hinges.

Sage was still at the window, moonlight framing her from behind. Candles of every shape and size flickered in the room. "Congratulations."

"Don't." Malcolm crossed to her. "No words." He stripped, pressed her against the wall, and pushed in. He ignored her whimper. He knew he should ease up, but he needed her. He needed to get into her and out of his head. He ignored her second whimper.

Sage pushed against him. "You said I'm not your whore, Malcolm. You're hurting **me**."

He eased up and let her pull herself free. Sage started to step around him. He took hold of her wrist to stop her, leaned her back against the wall again, "Sage. I'm sorry. I'm sorry. Lay with me, Girl. I'll do you right." Malcolm carried her to the bed, worked her tenderly — then buried himself deep.

~

Malcolm pulled Sage close and held her tight. "I'll be back on the fifth. You can stay at Oasis during the day, but make sure Luke or Sammi or Jason are nearby. Security will do check-ins with you if you're alone, and if they tell you to go to the ranch, make sure you go. Don't stay here at night, Sage."

"Except on the fifth, right? I can wait here for you to get back from Lewisburg, right?"

"Right."

"Because you have a surprise for me at the ranch, right?"

"Right." He pulled her close again, "Now lock up and put on security."

~

Malcolm inched toward the emergency vehicles stationed at the end of the pebble path. He stopped next to a local deputy, "What happened, Billy?" He forced himself to ask, though he already knew.

The young man shook his head, "A young woman ……. a young woman was murdered in her little cottage, Mr. Price. I'm **so sorry**, Mr. Price."

"How?" Malcolm choked.

"Stabbing. It must have been someone she knew. Someone raged that girl to death."

Malcolm heard the word "girl" and lost it.

The breaking man spins the Mercedes away from the picket fence, tears off of the pebble path and through Wyldwood toward his ranch. He storms into his stone and wood home and bellows, "SAMMI! JASON!"

The two race to the foyer arriving in time to see their boss storming across the second floor balcony-wrap. He calls over his shoulder, "Raise that fucking cottage. It'd better be gone by the next time I see either of you."

Across the pond.

Eighteen-year-old Manuel Xavier thinks he is flying below radar – he should know better. He is just about to pull his travel bag off the carousel at London's Heathrow Airport when he is approached by two security officers.

"Please step away from the conveyor and come with us."

"Why?"

"Step away and come with us."

The two officers flank him and several others move toward them. One retrieves Manuel's bag and falls in line behind the trio. No words are spoken until they get to a steel door at the far end of the terminal, "Step inside."

He does not move.

"Step inside."

With no choice but to obey, Manuel steps inside the empty room. One of his escorts drops his travel bag onto the floor, kicks it inside, closes the door, and flips the lock. For the first hour of his lockdown, he paces, he checks the door handle three times, he checks the other one across the room the same number of times, he takes wall space. He spends his second hour jogging in place, doing jumping jacks, pushups, and every other damn thing to work away his pent up frustration and energy. The third hour is spent with his butt on the floor and his back to a wall. He is on his feet and pacing the room when the door at the far end opens four hours into his confinement. "Should have known," he snarls when his father walks in.

"Si. It's good to see you – your return flight to New York leaves in an hour."

Manuel smiles wide showing off an amazing set of long, line dimples that are beginning to trench deep creases. "You wasted your money."

"If your plans are to abandon Juilliard without acquiring graduating credentials, then si, I have wasted my money."

Manuel smiles, "You know why I'm here."

Rocco closes the door, "I know you think there are discussions ahead of us. There are not."

Manuel laughs. "You have objections."

"Si. Many."

"Hold your objections until I have a chance to answer your questions."

"My questions will reveal my objections."

"I'm counting on that," Manuel laughs again.

Rocco nods, "You are off to a respectable start." The men take wall space across the room from one another.

"You are eighteen," the father begins.

"I'll establish residency in the U.K., go through prescreening and then submit my application. The review process from that point takes about a year."

"You are without a baccalaureate."

"I transferred my credits from Juilliard and Barnard to Columbia University. I have some course work to finish, but I'll graduate next year with a degree in computer science with a concentration in security, privacy and networking. I'll have to go back occasionally, but most of my work will be done remotely."

The father asks his next question in Italian.

The son answers the question in Italian and then in Spanish and then in English. "I speak three languages," he leans in, "two of them are romance languages. I find it helps with the ladies."

Rocco beams, then reigns in his enthusiasm and listens to his son.

"You are running down the requirements for the Secret Intelligence Service, so let me just cut to the quick."

Rocco nods.

"I am carrying a 4.0 from Columbia in computer science, and also from Barnard in economics. I have an extensive record of international travel, though the majority of it was under the name Manuel Duff which prohibits my declaration, but the head honcho at SIS knows all about my travels, so I doubt that'll be an issue. I am fluent in English, have an intermediate ability in Italian and Spanish, and a smattering of Portuguese…"

"Interesting choice," the father opines.

"There was a girl…"

"There always is."

"Si. Anyway, I will be transferring language studies from the International Foreign Language Institute of New York to its London branch as soon as you let me out of this fucking room." Manuel pushes off the wall and steps halfway toward his father, "And as for combat training; that will be on display if you don't let me out of this fucking room to take a piss."

Rocco pushes off the wall he's been riding and meets his son at the center point. "You'll have to work on your patience if you're going into the family business."

Manuel trenches *that* smile, "So you are on board?"

"No." Rocco Fiancetti cuffs his son's head from behind, pulls him close, and kisses his cheek. He turns toward the door – Then – Stops – Cold.

"I do my training in England under the watchful eye of the Inspector General of SIS. Or I do it in the United States under the watchful eye of the Director of the FBI."

The Senior Special Operative loses a bit of his patience. **"You will do no such thing, Manuel."**

"I will do my training at MI6 or at FICA. The choice is yours. And when I begin that training you will do nothing to impede my success."

"Nor will I do anything to ensure it."

Rocco opens the door to leave.

Manuel begins to follow.

"You cannot be seen with me, Manuel. You must find your own way now."

For five years, Manuel Xavier did a damned good job finding his own way. He went from applicant, to trainee, to top graduating recruit from Fort Monckton without hearing Word One from his father. He continued his stellar training record in the advanced physical and tactical components of IONEC, the unofficial spy school of the Secret Intelligence Service. When the graduate was summoned to the newly seated Inspector General's office, Manual Xavier expected an appointment to UKSF, the United Kingdom Special Forces training division.

Manuel reads the letter he'd been handed, "Quantico? I'm being sent for training at Quantico?"

Mick Bentley nods.

"You aren't offering me UKSF?"

"I am not."

"You aren't extending me a position at MI6?"

"I am not."

"Permission to speak freely?"

Mick Bentley pulls a long deep breath, "Quite sure I'll regret this, but speak freely, Mr. Xavier."

"Where is he?"

"Who?"

"The Senior Special Operative who I'm about to kill."

Mick moves from behind his enormous desk, "That right there is part of why you need to leave SIS. The two of you aren't cut well enough to work for the same country, let alone on the same mission."

"I'll offer a rebuttal to that point after I hear what the other part of your reasoning is."

"No one, so far as we know, has made a connection between Senior Special Operative Alistair Duff, and the MI6 trainee known as Manuel Xavier. If that connection is made it lands you both in grave danger. You will be hunted and used as a weapon against your father. You are his only Achilles heel, Manuel, and there are adversaries who would love nothing more than to bring the most valuable U.K. asset to his knees."

Manuel is silent for many minutes. When he stands he extends his hand to the man he's known his whole life, the one who raised him with The Duff, the one he considers to be his father, "Thank you, Mick. And if it's not too much trouble, tell Alistair Duff and Rocco Fiancetti to fuck off," he makes his way to the door and has his final say, "and tell him he shouldn't wear Aramis cologne."

Mick laughs as he pulls open an office door behind which stands Manuel's father. "Your son sniffed you out."

"Si. He is good."

Texas

Malcolm Price made it through those five years by punishing himself on the court or at the ranch. When he was playing the boards, he left every damn thing he had on the floor. He solidified his place as a future Hall of Famer, and he **became** 77 – because he just couldn't stand being Malcolm Price. When he was working his land, he spent more time in the saddle than there was in each day. The man needed the near break of exhaustion to get any rest — though it was only blood and bone that ever felt any relief.

During quiet times – though few and far between – Malcolm surrendered to the overwhelming feelings of guilt. He knew he played a role in what happened to Sage – in fact, he knew he played the starring role. No matter his intentions, he poked the bear and a beautiful girl named Sage Finley was mauled to death. She was the one who paid the price for one man's hubris and another man's vengeance.

The beginning of the end.

77 has done nothing more than take his morning shower when he parks his ass on the balcony of his hotel room in Miami, Florida. He listens to the talking heads on KZDS AM 724 in San Antonio.

Big mistake…

"San Antonio. Your team takes to the boards tonight for the first game of the 2013 NBA Finals. The question that's being asked across the great state of Texas is whether The Malcolm Price will lead Black and Silver to another Title…"

"…sorry to interrupt, Don, but if he can't do IT, who can? Every year since the young player donned team jersey 77 he's brought his team to the playoffs…"

"…sorry to interrupt, but let's give those listeners out there who might not know…or remember…a little recap of The Malcolm Price years…"

"…in 2003 he was the 28th round draft pick out of Bucknell University…"

"…and in his rookie season he brought the Spurs to the Finals…"

"…only to leave the playoffs with a fractured thumb which could have ended his career, but…"

"…he came back the next season and not only brought the Spurs to the playoffs they stood victorious at the end of play and took the 2005 Championship Title…"

"...then Price returned the following season and took the team to the playoffs..."

"...only to lose to Dallas in Game 7 of First Round play. The following year 77 was anointed with the esteemed title of The Malcolm Price after taking the Spurs to the Finals and beating LeBron James and the Cavs for the 2007 Title..."

"...and that series went a long way in helping the player assuage his ego gooood by going toe to toe and beating the 2003 1st round draft pick..."

"...right, and then came the 2007-2008 season .... the opening day only a few months after the brutal murder of Price's girlfriend, Sage Finley. Betting men and women across the state counted him out, but he..."

"...brought his team to the playoffs only to cede their Title bid to Dallas in Game 5 of First Round play. And from 2009 through 2012 The Malcolm Price has brought his team to the dance every year only to see them be sidelined from Final play..."

"...which brings us to tonight, San Antonio! Your team is back in the hunt for the 2013 NBA Championship Title, and all hopes are pinned on The Malcolm Price!"

Welcome to the 2013
NBA Championship
Finals

"It may be a beautiful balmy night outside the American Airlines Arena in Miami, Florida..."

"...but inside the packed arena, the Heat is rising as Miami gets ready to battle the San Antonio Spurs in Game 1 of the 2013 NBA Championship Finals..."

"...and don't forget the mano e mano battle between King James and The Malcolm Price..."

"...no one is forgetting *that* Don, certainly not the men, themselves. There's been a longstanding 'thing' between the players that seems to intensify during post-season play..."

"...so get ready because IT IS ON!"

San Antonio wins by 10.

"We're in Miami for Game 2 of this year's NBA Championship Finals. The San Antonio Spurs handed the Miami Heat their first loss by holding the team to a dozen fourth quarter points..."

"...which did not set well with the home team..."

"...which is expected to take the court tonight with a vengeance..."

Miami wins by 20.

"The Spurs are back home and tied with the Heat. The Malcolm Price looked good during warmups and is having relaxed conversation with his players..."

"...77 sure does look relaxed, Don, and if that's the case then he's the only one inside this Center who isn't feeling the Heat..."

"...damn straight...it feels like a powder keg in here..."

San Antonio wins by 33.

"The Malcolm Price dominated play two nights ago scoring..."

"...27 points in one of the most exciting games I've seen..."

"...and if he has another night like that..."

"...things will be looking gooood for the Spurs..."

Miami wins by 7.

"The teams are tied and the Spurs are looking for a win tonight so they have a series lead when they head back to Miami..."

"...and it sure would make things better for the Heat if they return home with the series lead..."

"...so..."

San Antonio wins by 10.

"Miami returns to American Airlines Arena behind in the series 3-2..."

"...but the King is back on his home Court..."

"and 77 much prefers playing in the Lone Star State..."

"...so..."

Miami wins in OT by 3.

"It is Game 7 and IT ALL COMES DOWN TO TONIGHT!"

"...what an amazing series this has been, Don. The play by these two teams could not be more similar. It's hard to find an edge for either team..."

"...and you'd be hard pressed to get me to call it either way..."

"...but Miami has home court advantage..."

"...and it paid off big last night, but..."

"...77 IS IN THE HOUSE..."

"...so..."

At the end of the first quarter – Miami is up by two. At the halftime buzzer – the teams are tied. At the end of the third quarter – Miami is up by a point. With seconds on the clock – Miami is ahead by three. 77 charges the court, takes the final shot, swishing a three-pointer for the tie —

then lands full body on the boards —
his knee absorbing the entire weight of
the man.

The crowd silences. Spurs players surround their injured leader. When they remove the legendary point guard on a stretcher, those in the bleachers and those watching from home fear they have witnessed the final play of The Malcolm Price. The morning headlines say it all.

Miami Heat: NBA Champs

Spurs lose more than a Title —
The Malcolm Price
played career ending game.

It's hot as Hell in Miami.

When Jason Carpenter arrives at Baptist Health Hospital he is met at the Information Desk by a security guard who travels with the Spurs. The guard steps in front of Jason.

"What's going on, Paddy?"

"Mr. Price is not accepting visitors."

"His choice. I'm not a visitor."

Paddy blocks Jason's path when he tries to move around him. "He's in bad shape, Jason. His knee is blown to shit. There's damage to all four collateral ligaments." He lets that information set. "77 is scheduled for surgery in the morning and when he's discharged, the Spurs are flying him on a private jet to San Antonio. He said to tell you he plans on staying at Alamo Heights."

Jason makes another move around Paddy who puts his hand onto the advancing man's chest. "I was asked to meet you, Jason. There's a security detail on the Orthopedic floor. You won't get in to see him. Let it go for tonight. I'm here for the duration and will be flying back with him. I'll call you as soon as I know anything."

Jason lowers and shakes his head. "His mother is…"

"Not welcome. Mr. Price is not accepting visitors."

"So you said." Jason swats Paddy's forearm away and storms out.

Lewisburg, Pennsylvania
Captain Damian Johnson pulls to the curb at the home of Bertha King Price. The woman he knows as Mama Girl moves from in front of the window and is standing at the door when Damian gets there.

"Thank you for coming Damian, and thank Wanda for letting her husband fly to Miami with..."

"Sorry to interrupt, Mama Girl, but Jason Carpenter called and said your son isn't accepting visitors. He asked that we not go to Miami."

Bertha does a bit of tsk-tsking, and head shaking. "It's Malcolm's way of things, Damian. He pushes people away when he needs them most."

"Yes, ma'am."

"Well sit yourself a bit and let's talk this through."

"Yes, ma'am."

It's even hotter in Wyldwood.

Three months after his career-ending injury, Malcolm Price returns to Wyldwood Ranch. He hasn't seen or spoken to Jason or Sammi since the Finals, and doesn't plan on doing much to rectify that. A tall order since they are all living under the same roof. Along for the ride, is the security guard who put Jason on notice in Miami. Paddy Stearns has been with Malcolm since they rolled him off center court on a stretcher and through some shit days thereafter. At Malcolm's request, Paddy left his job at the AT&T Center and has been with him round-the-clock since.

Jason and Sammi are nowhere near the main house when Malcolm arrives, and wait out two very long days before Paddy joins them downstairs.

"I'll keep you informed, but I won't jeopardize getting caught. Your friend is spiraling down. Right now, the only salvation he finds is at the dry end of a bourbon bottle. The booze is still working for him, but when he finishes the 77th bottle…"

"What?" Sammi blurts, "he brought 77 bottles of bourbon with him?"

Paddy nods, "Symbolic for something. Maybe that's gonna be his limit – finish bottle 77 then dry out, or…"

"…he'll move on to something stronger," Jason finishes Paddy's sentence.

After three months of 'hearing' about the descent of Malcolm Price, a broken Sammi calls Lewisburg for reinforcements and arranges an intervention at the ranch. The people who love Malcolm Price are waiting in the foyer when Paddy brings him back from an appointment in San Antonio.

Malcolm takes a quick look, turns around and begins his retreat from the ambush. Paddy stays firm in the doorway.

"Move."

"You should listen to them, Mr. Price."

"You should move." When Paddy crosses his arms and locks himself in place, Malcolm realizes he can't do much about him, but the people who've ambushed him – well he can do plenty about them. And. Then. He. Sees. Her. **"What the fuck, Sammi. You dragged Mama Girl into this mess!?"**

"I can't watch you destroy yourself, Malcolm."

"Then leave. Really, Sammi, get the fuck out!"

Mama Girl walks to her son and slaps him hard. "Looks like **you** dragged me into this mess, son. Don't go blaming other people for your self-pity or your self-loathing. Now since I'm here—you tell me I'm wrong to be—or accept that I am. Either way, Malcolm Price, pull yourself together."

Malcolm Price pulled himself up
and out of Texas.

Manuel Xavier returns to the U.S.

Recently appointed FBI Director, Shelby Webber, is waiting for FICA Assistant Director, Stacy Remington, to join her for a meeting. It should be noted that the meeting is not taking place at J. Edgar – far from it, actually. Shelby Webber is at her Arlington, Virginia, waterfront home, currently treading a path across gleaming hardwood floors. Her pacing takes her from corner to corner in front of floor to ceiling windows that overlook the Potomac River. The director, so deep in thought, makes no note of the view she loves. Rather, she is considering and reconsidering what she is about to do. A beep from a security panel at the far end of the room announces her guest's arrival and signals the end of her deliberation. "Showtime," Shelby says as she keys in a twelve-digit code that activates a wrought iron security gate through which Remington proceeds.

The director jogs down a set of stairs and exits her home just as her subordinate exits her vehicle. The Assistant Director, a generally brusque woman **not** prone to displays of — anything — does what everyone does when they take in the stately nineteenth century brick home and beautiful Potomac that moves just beyond the shoreline. She gasps and gawks.

"Permission to speak freely, Director?"

"Yes. And for the next hour or so I would like you to address me as Shelby."

There is a n.o.t.i.c.e.a.b.l.e. p.a.u.s.e. followed by an unsure nod and raised brow, "Very well, Shelllbeee." Stacy swallows that experience hard, "Well, that surely caused some internal discomfort, and I'm afraid it has displaced what I'd planned to say."

Shelby smiles wide, "I can imagine. I have a matter to discuss, AD Remington. It is a conversation that I will deny took place." She gives the AD a quick look then continues. "At this point in time, there are four people who know about an issue. If word were to get out, a) I will know that you leaked the information and b) covert assets will be unmasked. Take a few minutes enjoying the view and if you decide to assist with this matter, see yourself in."

Stacy doesn't take the offered time – she follows Shelby inside the three-story home and to a huge kitchen with a huge farmer's table.

"Take a seat Stacy."

The director attends a waiting coffee percolator, while Stacy's eyes settle on a view of the Potomac through a wall of windows.

"You take your coffee black, is that correct?"

"Yes, ma'am, Shelby, ma'am." Stacy shakes her head, "It's going to take a minute to adjust, Shelby."

Director Webber hands off a huge mug of coffee. "I've a bit to say, so you can just relax and listen. First and foremost, your direct supervisor, FICA Director, Roland Gaffney, **is not** part of this. He **is not** one of the four individuals who knows of this. He **will not** be told any of this."

Stacy nods.

Shelby continues.

"Gaffney is licking old wounds at having been passed over for the FBI director position – the position I hold. The individuals who sought my assistance insisted that he not be trusted with this issue. They determined he would question my participation and use it against me – no matter the relevance of my participation, or the jeopardy his interference might cause intelligence assets. I am in agreement with their assessment." Shelby does a final consideration over a sip of coffee, then wades in, "MI6 Senior Special Operative, Alistair Duff, is well known throughout cyber intelligence agencies."

"Yes."

"And throughout England because of his royal lineage."

"Yes."

"When Mick Bentley appointed Alistair to SIS in 1990, he made a public mention that Lady Frances Duff personally requested her son be given a chance at Monckton. That bit of taint caused most to consider Duff nothing more than an aristocrat who knows his way around a computer. In actuality, SSO Duff carries the same cover status as FICA's John Maxwell and Joy Ann Watts." Shelby studies Stacy for a 'tell' – so far, there is no tell. She continues. "Duff has several aliases, but his most covert alias, is Rocco Fiancetti."

The corner of Stacy's lips turn upward – ever so slightly. Shelby notices. Given that Stacy Remington – Does. Not. Smile. – Director Webber feels confident she found the AD's tell, and that her subordinate *knows* something about SSO Duff's alias.

Shelby gives a slight nod and continues. "Rocco Fiancetti is an unparalleled SIS cyber intelligence asset, but he is also the most effective clandestine operative the Inspector General has." Shelby lets that settle while she takes the empty mugs to the sink, grabs two more and fills them to the brim. She begins talking on her way back to the table. "Everything I told you is classified, of course, but more importantly it is background information."

Stacy sits up straighter in her seat and puts her mug onto the table, "That's some deep background, Shelby."

"In 1990, Alistair Duff had a son and gave custody of that child to his mother who, aided by boarding schools throughout Europe, raised young Manuel Duff until her death in 2003. At that time, the teen was removed from his life, given a new name, and removed from Europe. His existence was essentially scrubbed. Manuel Duff is legally known as Manuel Xavier, is a recent graduate of Columbia University, and SIS training academies. His records, however, show that he is a recent graduate of Columbia University and Quantico. Technically, he is both of those things. Manuel Xavier spent the past 18 months working in the FBI and CIA cyber facilities in Virginia, and is a soon-to-be applicant at FICA. I want him in the hacker-for-hire division. Make sure he gets greenlighted by Quadrant Manager, Kristen Millie."

"Consider it done."

"You will be his contact and conduit to me."

Stacy nods.

"Make no mistake on this point Stacy, Manuel Xavier will be an extremely valuable asset to the Agency. This is a very good hire."

"Yes, ma'am."

J. Edgar Hoover

Kristen Millie, hands several files to Agent Manuel Xavier. He reads the name at the top of the first file, "Wendell 'Stoner' Strong."

"Mr. Strong is a hacker-for-hire in Texas. He lives in San Antonio, but works statewide. He's been on our radar since 2007 when he did a deep dive on Malcolm Price. FICA Director Gaffney ordered that no victim notification be made while Price and the Spurs were in the hunt for the NBA Title. That decision has caused me some sleepless nights."

"How so?"

"Stoner Strong's uncle is Micky Strong."

"Ma'am?"

"Micky Strong was a PI in the San Antonio area. More to the point, he is being sought for the murder of Sage Finley, the former girlfriend of Malcolm Price. Familiarize yourself with the files Agent Xavier, then pack your bags. You're going to San Antonio for the duration. Do not come back to DC until Wendell 'Stoner' Strong is behind bars. I'll toss in a month's vacation if you can get Micky Strong."

"On it, ma'am."

It's about time.

The man known worldwide as The Malcolm Price left Texas in 2013, and took up residence in Vancouver, British Columbia. The day he arrived, he shaved his head, grew some facial scruff, rented a condo in the historic district of Gastown, and set about surviving from one day to the next. The guilt-ridden, self-loathing man did his surviving blind drunk, and in the beds of a whole bunch of women — **until** he woke next to one who had waist-length, stick-straight, black-as-coal hair, big, expressive eyes, and a wide, toothy smile. He pulled his ass from that bed, locked himself inside his condo for as many months as it took to dry himself out, and set about surviving from one night to the next.

Three hundred and sixty-five nights sober, Malcolm Price celebrates with a call to the guy he's known since grade school. "Damian."

"It's about time, brother."

"Yeah."

"You good?"

"I'm better. Tell Mama Girl you heard from me."

Another three hundred and sixty-five days later, "Damian."

"This our thing now?"

"Yeah."

"How many more anniversary calls will I be getting?"

"I'm working on some stuff that should take about a year. I'll surface after that. If you need to contact me, I'm in Vancouver."

"Gastown's a beautiful place to live."

"Shit, man. How long have you known?"

"Not long."

"How is Mama Girl?"

"Missing you."

"Yeah."

Damian Johnson disconnected from that call with a heavy heart. What he should have told his best friend was that Mama Girl needed her son and he'd better get his shit together and come home.

Almost home.

Sammi and Jason are finishing breakfast when a call comes from the security gate at the thoroughfare, "Mr. Price is approaching the main house."

They make their way to the foyer, arriving seconds before a very changed Malcolm Price drops his bags inside the front door.

"You two freeloaders are still here? Should'a changed the damn locks." He smiles w.i.d.e.

"We thought you were dead, so we put a homestead claim on this place," Jason smiles w.i.d.e.

Malcolm tilts his head in Sammi's direction, "Bet that was the real estate agent's idea."

She smiles. Sort of.

Malcolm approaches – slowly. "Sammi. You are a good woman. You are a better friend and am indebted. I'm sorry I caused you worry and that I hurt you."

Sammi falls into the arms he opens to her. When she gathers herself she gets down to business, "Are you hungry."

"You know it."

"Come on, I'll make you a Western."

"Like no one else can."

While Sammi cooks, the men step outside. There are many silent minutes before Malcolm speaks. "I'm leaving tomorrow. I can't be here. I don't want to be here."

Jason takes a hip-rest along the porch railing, "Do you want to sell the place?"

"Never." He takes a look toward the small hill where he laid to rest his Girl and her Momma. "This place is for Sage – and for you and Sammi. I'm hoping you will stay here, work the place, and make it your own."

"Already told you, we homesteaded the place."

Malcolm laughs big then settles some, "I appreciate your friendship, Jason. I am a better man for having known you."

Jason gets up and walks past his friend, "I'm glad you aren't dead."

"Me, too."

Sammi finds Malcolm standing at Sage's office door the next morning. "You should have left yesterday."

He starts laughing, "Why's that?"

"There's an FBI agent downstairs. He said he's here about Sage."

"Shit."

FICA Agent, Manuel Xavier, is waiting in the foyer for Malcolm Price. After an introduction he points to luggage that is set at the front door, "Are you coming or going, Mr. Price?"

Malcolm laughs, "I haven't been here in years. I show up. You show up. I'm sure you know the answer to your question. But since you asked, I'm going home."

"To Lewisburg."

"Why are you here, Agent Xavier?"

"An internet hacker-for-hire named Stoner Strong did a deep dive on you during the 2007 playoffs. Did you know anything about that, Mr. Price?"

"Not until Detective Romney mentioned it during his questioning of me in 2007."

"Any idea why the nephew of Micky Strong had a fascination with you?"

"You know the answer to that question, Agent Xavier. I think we're done, here. Correction: I'm done."

Home.

Shortly before nightfall Captain Damian Johnson meets Malcolm's flight. This time he arrives in his Land Rover and waits at the pick-up curb at Fox Hollow Airport. "Good to see you, brother."

"Same."

"Toss your things into the back. I've been given strict orders to bring you to Mama Girl's straight away."

"Better do it then."

Damian eyes a duffle bag at Malcolm's feet, "What's with the flower-power girly bag?"

Malcolm laughs, "It's Sammi's. She's been collecting my mail and stuffing it in that bag."

"Damn, it's packed full. Ought to take some time getting through that."

"Not sure I'll have much time."

"Why is that?"

"Drive a bit."

"Okay, but you're taking Mama Girl's wrath."

"Deal," he smiles that Malcolm smile. "I just finished a master's program at UPenn in Government and Public Policy."

"No shit?"

"I did most of it through correspondence courses, and some of it at Simon Fraser University in Vancouver."

"You planning on a career in politics?"

"Yes, but I need your help."

"Name it."

"I need a job."

Captain Johnson eyed his friend as though he'd lost his mind—or his memory. "You do know that you're a multi-gazillionaire, right?"

"I do."

"But you want a job?"

"I do."

"Where?"

"Lewisburg Penitentiary."

The End

More to come …

Please enjoy the teaser for my next book in the series,

Rescues…

RESCUES

THE HITMAN

--- PULLING THREADS ---

Book Eight

SHERYLL O'BRIEN

From paradise to prison.

U.S. Bureau of Prisons inmate BOP-PA-555925 is locked in a cell and gripped by a nightmare…

"You are American?" he asked the naturally pretty, strawberry-blonde woman sitting across from him on the near-empty first-class flight heading to Belize.

"Born in Paris, raised in America, and until very recently living again in Paris, and you?"

"Sort of," he said with a wide smile.

"A man of mystery," she said with a toss of her soft shoulder-length ringlets.

He liked the way her slightly upturned, freckled nose crinkled when she smiled wide. He particularly liked her light, easy way. "Are you vacationing in Belize?"

"Yes, and you?"

"Sort of," he said with a wide smile.

"The mystery continues," she chuckled.

"The Mayan ruins, is that your fascination with Belize?" he asked.

"Yes, of course, but the Belize Barrier Reef is my true fascination. I've heard the watering of Belize is like no other."

"Watering?"

Her laugh was free, infectious. "Snorkeling, scuba diving, rafting, kayaking, that sort of thing."

"A woman of watering? Never would have guessed it," he smiled.

She raised her glass of white wine in mock toast. "Guess I'm a woman of mystery, too," she laughed—a wonderful laugh.

~

"Love the treehouse," he said as he started toward the outside staircase. He stopped at the landing, waiting for his companion to head up. She was nowhere in sight.

"Over here, Manuel."

He turned toward her call and watched as she made her way up a rope ladder that was affixed to a nearby tree, as she pressed her back tight against the trunk, and as she pushed into a standing position. She unfurled a length of rope hooked to the side, grabbed it high, wrapped the ends tightly around her hands, pushed off, the momentum swinging her and bringing her to the building he thought they'd be entering in a more ordinary fashion. He smiled w.i.d.e. "I see watering isn't your only form of physical fitness."

"Get your ass up here, and I'll show you what else I can do."

~

Dominique was startled when Manuel dropped onto the first-class seat next to her. "What are you doing? I thought you left—because you needed to get back for your job?"

"I said I had something to do for work. I didn't say I was leaving Belize."

She furrowed her brow and tilted her head. "But you took your things."

"In case I couldn't get back before *you* left." He took hold of her hand and gave it a gentle squeeze. "I took care of what needed to be done and went back to the treehouse at Hamanasi. You were gone. I thought you were staying another few days, maybe another week."

The beautiful sun-kissed cheeks of the freckle-faced woman reddened and held the heat of the moment. "I... I..." she sighed and stared out the plane's window. "A month's vacation was enough. It's time to move on," she said over her shoulder.

Manuel stood, reached into his pocket, and sat back down. Dominique turned and watched his movements—she wished she hadn't when he showed her the pregnancy test he found discarded back at Hamanasi. "I think we have things to discuss, Dominique."

Surprise then upset flashed and settled on her face. "You shouldn't..."

"No, Dominique, you shouldn't."

ABOUT THE AUTHOR

She is not dead.

Sheryll O'Brien crafts characters without constraints. She tells them who they are, then let's them show her better versions of themselves. She gives them life and they live it beyond her wildest dreams.

Sheryll is a lifelong resident of Worcester, Massachusetts, where she is wife to the most supportive husband ever, and mother of two adult daughters, one who refuses to leave her home and the other who refuses to tell her where she lives. Of most significance, she is MammyGrams to the sweetest six-year-old, Hadley.

Sheryll worked several years in the fundraising community of Worcester County, writing grants for non-profit organizations. She began writing for her own pleasure after surviving brain surgery and breast cancer. Happily, for her fanbase of family and friends-—she is not dead.

If you have enjoyed reading my book, I would very much appreciate you taking a few minutes to write a review and post that review on amazon.com and goodreads.com.

The opinion of readers can help prospective readers make a purchasing decision.

To learn more, please visit my website, www.pullingthreadsnovella.com subscribe to my blog for updates on future projects.

I would absolutely love to hear from my readers, you can email me at,

pullingthreadsnovella@gmail.com